HOLLOW & VENOM

A POISONED KINGDOMS NOVEL

AMELIA MACLEOD

CONTENT NOTES

Note: Skip this note if you prefer not to read content warnings.

Hollow & Venom contains themes that may be upsetting to some readers.

These include: the threat of sexual assault; self harm (under compulsion); parental abuse of a child (memories); murder; and fantastical violence/battles.

There is also a strong element of human enthrallment or compulsion, which amounts to a form of slavery. None of the sympathetically portrayed characters utilize or sanction this power without permission.

This book also contains explicit sex scenes.

Take care of yourselves while reading, my friends.

Sincerely,
Amelia

CHAPTER ONE

NEVE

*T*he fortress smelled of frying dough and cinnamon, and not in a good way.

Sugar coated the back of Neve's throat as she passed the outer walls, choking back the sensation of having stepped into a pastry oven. Every breath was a cloying, caramel-infused mess, the warm air making it difficult to fill her lungs to a satisfying degree.

The courtyard teemed with activity, humans trotting by with baskets of food, heaps of tablecloths, or plates stacked to their ears. Ladders dotted the interior walls and balconies as humans reached to hang floral garlands.

A mage could have done any of this work, all of it, with the flick of a finger. Yet the humans did it all with smiling ease, resentment the furthest thing from their minds. As if they were preparing this festival for themselves. As if they would be the ones to enjoy the confections, the dancing, the holiday.

Fighting a sneeze, Neve moved deeper into the courtyard, tucking a strand of her short dark hair behind her ear as she fell into step behind a human servant who was hefting three bags of flour. It was easy to join the crowd. Easy to look like she belonged.

Here and there, a few of the mages watched from the multitude of dark-wood balconies that extended from the upper floors of the interior fortress. She didn't look at them long enough to catch their expressions, but she had no doubt they were watching for their own twisted amusement.

They wouldn't be on the lookout for a rogue human. As far as they knew, no such thing existed.

Still, she had to remind herself of that as she wound her way across the expansive courtyard, aiming for the interior halls of the fortress. It was hard to remember to breathe easily, especially when each inhalation stung her nostrils with burned sugar.

If only the fortress were near the sea. If only a salty breeze could whip through these walls to dispel the sugary fog. Fresh and hearty, and real.

Soon. Soon, she would be there. As long as she did not fail today.

Still, she was so caught up with the vision of breaking waves and pearl-white sand that she forgot to watch where she was going, even as she headed deeper inside the fortress. Even as she passed into the cool shade of its interior walls. Into the heart of the mages' power.

When the woman in front of her slowed, hitching one of four baskets higher onto her hip as she tried to maintain her grip, Neve had to dart to the side to keep from slamming into her. The basket slipped, and Neve lunged to catch it, throwing her arms around it just in time. The cursed thing was so heavy it nearly threw off her own balance, but she managed to hold on. Barely.

"Thank you, miss," the woman said. "What a stroke of luck that you happened to be there."

Had the contents of that basket spilled within sight of a

mage, the punishment would have been severe. Of course, that was what they would be hoping for. They lived for punishable mishaps. The basket was too bulky, piled high with apples, oranges, and pears, and there was no reason this woman should be carrying four of them at once.

Mages clearly didn't believe in carts.

And yet, the woman was smiling, a sparkle in her eye that made Neve's throat tighten. It wasn't real. None of it was real.

"Let me help you," Neve said.

"I'd be most grateful." The woman swiped a strand of gray hair out of her eyes, still smiling. But her dress hung off her figure, as if she'd once filled it with more ample curves, and her shoes were worn down to such an extent that visible holes rubbed against the cobblestones. She must end every day with blisters on her heels.

The woman handed her a second basket, and together they ducked into the dim halls of the fortress.

"Wish they'd hold a festival every year, instead of every three," the woman said as they made their way through the hall. "But then, I s'pose it's a lot of preparation. And there's nothing like anticipation. Last time, there were the fireworks. Were you here for that? They were stunning. I wonder if they'll do it again."

Neve's heart twisted. She'd rather spend the rest of her days miserable than feel fake happiness the mages had implanted in her brain.

She swallowed a wad of bile. "I do remember the fireworks."

The woman chuckled. "Romantic, aren't they? All those shapes and colors. I've been dreaming of them ever since."

Neve wanted to scream at the woman, to shake her until her senses returned, but it would do no good. They were deep in the fortress and surrounded by mages. There was nowhere in the Vales that the thrall was stronger.

One pouch of coins, and Neve would be gone.

She'd nearly saved enough to book passage to the Etran Islands. A month, maybe two, and she'd be gone. And then, just yesterday, she'd overheard the apothecary, Lydia, saying she'd pay a heap of coins for a live shimmerling. Neve ran errands and deliveries for her upon occasion, and Lydia had been talking to her assistant, not realizing that Neve was in earshot.

Shimmerlings were rarely found in the wild anymore. Native to the Vales, the little lizards now existed only for the mages to abuse. Just like everything and everyone else. There were many reasons an apothecary might want to have a closer look at one.

Neve had tossed and turned through the night, unable to think of anything else. If she brought Lydia a shimmerling, she could be free now. Tonight.

Except that there was nowhere to *get* a shimmerling. Nowhere but the castle.

And so here she was. Preparing to steal from an entire palace full of powerful tyrants. It was enough to make her want to drop her baskets and run.

Once she was off, she reminded herself, she would never have to look back. Mages lived in Etra, too—they lived everywhere in the Vales—but the country was far more remote.

Secrets would be easier to keep.

Neve followed the woman around a corner, where the hall opened into a hexagonal antechamber. A trio of corridors branched out from it, including the one they'd come from. The first corridor was empty.

But the one on the far side of the antechamber was occupied by a mage.

He lounged in a cushioned window seat, watching something in the passage ahead. Recognizable as much by his bored expression as by the fine tunic he wore, the golden stitches in his shoes, and the otherworldly shimmer that seemed to hang in the surrounding air. Thankfully, he appeared to be too occupied with something further down the hall to notice their arrival. Neve couldn't see what could have captured his attention so fully, but she doubted she would wish to.

The remainder of the antechamber was piled with flowers and food, the heady scent of the blooms mixing with fruit and sugar, and an inexplicable whiff like the singe of a snuffed candle. Her companion headed directly to a table that was already groaning with overloaded fruit baskets. Neve didn't think there were enough mages in all the Vales to eat that fruit before it spoiled. Let alone the bread and pastries being prepared somewhere below.

"Thank you, dear," the human woman said. "Saved me a world of trouble, if you didn't know."

Neve swallowed hard. She did know. "Can you point me to the west tower? I'm meant to go there next."

Supposedly, the prince kept his shimmerlings there. During the festival, the lizards would be butchered, and he would enchant their bones to create relics that would maintain the mages' hold on humans throughout the Vales.

"West tower," the woman repeated, the question half-formed on her lips. What errand could possibly have Neve flitting in that direction?

But the woman merely pointed toward the passage that was occupied by the bored mage, her hand shaking just a touch. Perhaps she thought she'd delayed one of the prince's own servants. "Entrance is that way. I've held you from your task long enough. Run along."

Of *course* the entrance had to take her by the mage in the window. Of course. She wanted to try and circle back around, find another route. But the woman was still watching, and Neve could hardly pretend she'd misspoken.

Enthralled humans didn't misspeak. They didn't change their minds. And they definitely didn't avoid corridors merely because they were occupied by mages.

Feeling suddenly bereft without a basket to clutch, Neve started for the passage, trying to ignore the mage. But it was impossible not to follow his half-lidded gaze to the passage ahead. To where a human man and woman sat on crates before a makeshift dining table, feasting on a platter of hot coals.

Neve's feet slowed without her permission as the human man used a pair of delicate tongs to select a glowing coal from the top of the pile. He popped it into his mouth, closing his eyes with a blissful smile as his teeth crunched the hot cinder.

"Unmatched," he said. "Absolutely divine."

His lips were puffed with blisters, some of them blackened and oozing. When a trickle of blood streamed from the corner of his mouth, he used a lace napkin to dab it away.

Horror stopped Neve in her tracks as the man's companion bobbed her head in agreement, snatching up her own piece of coal with bare, blistered fingers.

The mage in the window chuckled. He'd flattened his straw-yellow hair against the top of his head in a style so slick it looked like it could be a cap. Or the hard shell of a beetle. He'd obviously chosen his clothing to accentuate that feature, though Neve couldn't begin to guess why. It could hardly be called a color at all, leeched and lifeless as it was.

A second mage watched from the other side of the corridor, amusement sparkling in her eyes. She wore a jade-green dress, the silky hem kissing the stones of the floor. How she could walk in it without tripping, Neve could not begin to guess.

In other parts of the Vales, and at other times, the enthrallment that the mages placed on humans was no more than a vague sort of listlessness. Humans—hollows, as the mages called them—lived their lives more or less on their own paths. Mages were far fewer than humans, and they preferred the amusements of the cities to the quiet of the rural countryside.

The shimmerling relics kept people docile when there weren't as many mages around. This festival, which came every three years, was their method of handing out recharged relics. The thrall didn't last forever. That, Neve knew better than anyone.

"So kind of you," the human woman said, the coal still clasped between her fingertips. When the thrall lifted, even slightly, she would wake to find herself in agony. No doubt these mages would want to be there to witness that part, too. "So kind of you to let us join the festivities early."

The mage in the window laughed again.

"West tower's up the stairs, right that way." Neve jumped as the human woman she'd helped came bustling by, a newly empty basket in her hands. She jutted her chin toward the nearest stone staircase, pointing the way. If she saw the grotesque feast her fellow humans were sharing, she didn't let on.

Neve could do nothing to help them. She just needed to snatch her shimmerling and get out. Even though it suddenly felt impossibly foolish to steal anything from the mages. But this was her path, already chosen. If she turned away now, they'd begin to suspect.

So, to the west tower she would go.

Up the stairs she climbed, one hand on the rough wall. Her own skirts might not trail on the floor, but she lifted them just the same, giving her feet their best chance of keeping their balance on the uneven steps.

When she reached the first landing, she paused, catching her breath against the windowsill. Sunset was in full bloom now, spilling orange and fuchsia beams across the staircase. On the garden side, the flowers glowed as if they, too, planned to sink beneath the horizon for the night.

Perhaps mages' flowers did that. What did Neve know?

She continued on.

The stairs were empty, at least compared with the busyness

below. Even the sugar-drenched scent had eased somewhat, allowing a draft of fresh air to circulate through the stairwell.

A minute passed, and another. The orange of the sunset faded to pink, leaving smears of blue behind. Candles on the wall flared to life as if summoned.

She was close now. She *had* to be close.

A bright flash of color caught her gaze to the left, shining from beneath the next iron doorway. With a steadying breath, Neve pushed the door open.

Inside the room there stood a cage, a wooden hutch filled with tiny glowing creatures, their scales combining into an iridescent rainbow of greens, pinks, purples, and blues. Together, they shone so brightly that the room was fully lit, even without any lamps.

"Shimmerlings," she breathed. For all their infamy, she'd never laid eyes on a live one. No larger than the length of her index finger, the lizards moved with striking speed. Up the walls of the hutch, pressed to the ceiling, scurrying along the floor. There were so many.

Neve pressed her free hand to the netting. A blue shimmerling made its way over, flicking its tongue toward her, tasting the air. *Friend or foe?* It seemed to ask.

When the festival began, these shimmerlings would be sacrificed in a blaze of magefire. They would die, the prince would corrupt their bones with some spell, and humans throughout the Vales would be freshly enthralled.

They called him the Soulslayer—the prince, that was, not the lizards—though no one quite knew how he'd earned the title. Just before she'd come to Vunmore, about six years ago, he'd disappeared. When he reappeared three years later, the whispers said, he'd become the most powerful mage in generations. No one knew how or why, at least among the humans.

The blue shimmerling flicked out its tongue again, and Neve decided.

8

She couldn't take this creature and subject it to whatever fate Lydia had in mind for it. And she couldn't save just one. Not now that she'd seen them.

The latch was easy to undo. No lock, no spell, no wardings whatsoever. Mages were nothing if not overconfident about what was theirs.

And why shouldn't they be? As far as Neve had ever been able to learn, she was the only person in all the Vales who was immune to the spell of the thrall.

Before she could think better of it, she pushed the latch aside and flung the door open, releasing a torrent of glowing lizards into the night. "Be free."

Rough hands grabbed her from behind, hauling her out of the shimmerling room and into the hall. "Now, little hollow," said the yellow-haired mage from the corridor as she kicked, scrambling uselessly for purchase. "Just what do you think you're doing?"

CHAPTER TWO

SYLVAN

*S*ylvan would have preferred to hold the interrogation in his own chambers, where the darkness allowed him to control the perceived passage of time. Here in his brother's tower, shreds of sunlight pierced the windowpanes like flares, bathing the room in fistfuls of bloody light. Though perhaps that was a fancy of Sylvan's imagination, given what was about to happen here.

His brother leaned against the arched window, silhouetted against the red-orange light. Broad-shouldered and strong from the pointless sword-waving he insisted on practicing, Thorne was the picture-perfect image of what a prince ought to be. Strong-jawed and golden-haired, his clothing brushed down and free of wrinkles, his shoes polished to a blinding shine.

In comparison, Sylvan was a monster in the dark.

Thorne's arms were crossed, his expression neutral, but each time he tightened his hands into fists—a squeeze, a hold, a release—he betrayed the emotions that rushed beneath the surface. Thorne was the elder brother, yet he still needed the most practice in hiding his feelings. They roiled on the surface, all too obvious: a slice of fear at what had almost happened here and, crucially, more than a little rage.

Sylvan flicked his attention away from his brother to focus on the intruder. The mage's limbs were flattened against the arms of the chair, Sylvan's power hardening the air around him into an impenetrable cage. Ropes were only as good as the one who tied them—or the one who checked for secret knives hidden in sleeves—but hardened air would not let the captive twitch a thumb, let alone withdraw a knife.

It could even smother breath itself, if Sylvan wanted it to. And for the last thirty seconds or so, he had very much wanted it to. The man's aura was a splash of sickly greenish-gold, flickering around his head like a dying light. His eyes were bloodshot, the lids held open by Sylvan's magic.

It would be a mercy to end the mage now. Unfortunately for him, Sylvan wasn't feeling all that merciful.

"Honestly, Sylvan, assassination attempts are practically a weekly occurrence," Thorne said. "There's no need to be so dramatic."

Had Sylvan not been so practiced at concealing his reactions, he'd have rolled his eyes. If Thorne really believed that, he'd have called King Asperion's guards to arrest the man.

Instead, he had summoned Sylvan. And he knew exactly what Sylvan's brand of justice would entail.

Sylvan eased his hold on the captive, allowing a trickle of breath to reach the man's nostrils while still holding him immobile. The man wheezed, but Sylvan allowed him no relief. He propped one hand on the back of the chair and leaned in, close enough to smell the mage's rancid breath.

"I will ask you again," Sylvan said. "Who sent you to kill my brother?"

The assassin had the audacity to laugh. No more than a sliver of air for his starved lungs, and the fool used it to *laugh*. "You claim him as brother?" The assassin wasn't looking at

Sylvan; his eyes, watery with pain, were focused on Thorne. "Everyone knows that Sylvan Everstone is a bastard of your mother's."

Thorne blinked lazily, but the flash of anger was all too obvious behind his attempt to hood his gaze. "Which, were it true, would still make him my brother. Imbecile."

Unlike Thorne, Sylvan was well practiced at concealing his emotions. For the past six years, he'd focused on it almost to the exclusion of all else, hardening himself until his shell was more scales than skin, every tender point shuttered behind thick layers of armor.

They thought him a monster. So, a monster he would be.

He still had emotions, naturally; even the sharpest magic could not burn them away entirely. But to give in to them was a weakness Sylvan could not afford, and so he kept them locked safely away, safely controlled, where they could not be used against him.

Thorne moved away from the window and draped himself on the cushioned settee in the corner, his long legs dangling off the end in a way that could not truly be comfortable. Around his neck, he wore a vial containing a small amount of the sacred magepool water that tied them to their home world. Sylvan didn't know how his brother could keep the stuff so close to his skin; he wore his own vial tied to a loop at his belt.

He'd do away with it entirely if he could.

"With that red hair of yours," the assassin wheezed, once again daring to address Sylvan directly, "they say your mother lay with the Demon himself."

Thorne tsked. "I take it back. There is a need to be dramatic."

Sylvan brushed his fingertip against his thumb, relishing the way the power sparked to life against his skin. Magefire, at his disposal and begging for release. For six years he had commanded it—and so many other powers—yet the ability still felt new. It still felt... unwieldy. As if the slightest twitch might ignite the fortress in a shower of sparks.

Sylvan relished it. "You've one more chance for a merciful death," he said. "I suggest you take it."

The assassin wheezed again, a wet choke of a sound. "How did you truly survive three years in the Miragelands, Soulslayer? They say it's because the demons recognized you as kin."

Bold words, but Sylvan recognized them for what they were: a last-ditch attempt to prod at his emotions. To provoke him into making a mistake. As if the majority of his armor were not artfully constructed around the issue of his mother.

What they never seemed to understand? Sylvan was *glad* King Asperion, fool that he was, was not his father. He was glad to be a bastard.

He glanced at Thorne, who'd propped one hand behind his head. To his credit, he had not shut his eyes. He would face the flavor of justice he'd chosen to summon. He met Sylvan's gaze and nodded.

Bracing one knee on the seat of the chair, Sylvan leaned over the assassin, fingers itching with heat. He needed no blades. "You come for my brother, you come for me."

The assassin spat. "Your brother is weak. And you are weaker still."

Rage heated Sylvan's gut, but he forced it down and away, channeling power into his hands. With the gentleness of a lover, he pressed his palm against the man's exposed throat.

The assassin's upper lip curled into a sneer, head tilted back against the pressure of Sylvan's touch. He still thought he could withstand it, this little bit of discomfort. This little bite of pain. Like the rasp of a shallow cut, the sting of a summer wasp.

It always began that way.

Sylvan delved. The man's heartbeat was a beacon in the dark, erratic and lizard-like though it was, and Sylvan's magic latched on, riding the uneven tide through every artery, vein, and capillary, through every crease of skin, every follicle of hair, every corner of every organ—the kidneys, the lungs, the roiling stomach—until the very blood within the man's vessels sang with Sylvan's power.

Sweat beaded on the assassin's forehead, and he squirmed as Sylvan stepped back, folding his arms. His aura spilled into the air, mixing with the assassin's, and Sylvan no longer needed to touch him to invade his every pore.

When every part of the man was full to bursting, Sylvan twisted the power into magefire.

The assassin screamed as his blood began to boil, blisters erupting across his neck, his face, his hands. The smell of burned flesh filled the room, mixing with the brine of blood, until it was all that existed. Until he was more inferno than man.

As abruptly as it had begun, the screaming stopped. The man slumped in his chair, the thrum of his pulse gone still.

Thorne unfolded himself from the settee, coming to stand beside Sylvan. He surveyed the scene, one eyebrow ticked. "Just because you can, brother, doesn't mean you should."

Sylvan pushed his tongue against the roof of his mouth, biting back a sharp retort. If the assassin couldn't prompt an emotional reaction out of him, then his brother certainly shouldn't be able to. And yet sometimes, Sylvan found it more difficult to channel the irritation away when Thorne was the source of it.

"If you object to my methods, then summon the guard next time." He could taste blood on his tongue, as thick and metallic as his victim's. But sweet, too, honeyed by the spell of the magefire.

He rubbed his fingertips together, annoyed with Thorne, and with himself. Perhaps there was a shred of truth in his brother's words. He *had* lost a grain of his control. For an instant only, but the knowledge of it sat heavy in his gut.

Control was strength, and Sylvan needed every ounce he could muster.

The door opened, and Sylvan's human valet, Flint, peered into the room. He wore spectacles on the end of his long nose, and Sylvan always wondered what good they could do him from down there. He suspected the man wore them merely so he could raise his bushy eyebrows and peer over the rims.

"Screaming stopped," Flint observed. "Are you finished then?"

As if he were asking whether they'd completed a meal, rather than a murder. Sylvan pulled on his gloves. "This mess isn't yours, Flint. I'll take care of it."

Flint clucked his tongue and hurried into the room, his cleaning bag slung over his shoulder. "You never scrub hard enough. Gets between the cracks and stains." He waved his hands, practically shooing them toward the door.

Sylvan had the distinct impression that the man was kicking them out of Thorne's rooms.

Thorne watched as the man began his work. "Is it not dangerous to leave your humans un-enthralled?"

Sylvan retrieved his cloak from where he'd thrown it on the chair hours ago. "Flint," he said, "would you betray me?"

Flint extracted a cleaning solution from his bag. If it was the one Sylvan recognized, Thorne's rooms would smell like mint and acid for a week. A price Thorne deserved. "No, sir. You pay well, and you assign fascinating tasks."

If Sylvan didn't know better, he would think the man *enjoyed* these 'tasks.' "I didn't assign that one," Sylvan pointed out. "You waited outside the door for it."

"Nevertheless, sir. Nevertheless."

Sylvan looked at Thorne. "You see? Perfectly safe."

Thorne opened the door and stepped onto the landing. "If I were an un-enthralled human, that's precisely what I would say. Right before I throttled you in your sleep."

16

Sylvan wanted to reply that it would be no less than he deserved, that monsters begat monstrous deaths. But Thorne would argue or make a quip. And Sylvan was in no humor for arguments, and even less for jokes.

"Is that why you keep no human servants yourself?" Sylvan asked him.

Thorne winced. "Perhaps."

"I'm far more concerned about who is sending mage assassins to kill you in your bed," Sylvan said. "I hope you plan to inform the king."

Thorne shrugged. "I suppose I must. He'll hear talk in any case."

"Flint will say nothing," Sylvan said.

"I wasn't thinking about Flint."

"Who else then?"

Thorne clapped a hand on Sylvan's shoulder. "Possibly everyone in the fortress, given the volume of those screams. I wasn't alone when the villain arrived to slit my throat."

Sylvan frowned. "All your charms, and you cannot persuade a single woman to keep a secret?"

"A single woman, perhaps," Thorne said, running his fingertips along the rail. "But all three? Unlikely."

And Thorne worried about the humans Sylvan refused to enthrall. "You allow half the population into your bed. No wonder assassins find it easy to access you."

"The more the merrier," Thorne replied. "As long as they leave their knives at the door."

Thorne could act as flippant as he liked; Sylvan knew that he was shaken by the attack. Angry, too. He'd have called the guards, otherwise.

Sylvan wanted to believe that the king would investigate. But the man was a fool of the highest order, a jester in a crown. It would depend entirely on his mood and his focus at the moment. He was just as likely to laugh it off and celebrate

Thorne's victory over the assassins as he was to worry, increase the guard, and order his spies to investigate the attack.

Still, Thorne was his heir. The only one of his sons who pleased him, despite his relentless dalliances. Sylvan sometimes thought King Asperion was most proud of the dalliances. Even more than the sword waving.

The king acknowledged Sylvan only because he had to. Because the most powerful mage in generations could not be ignored.

Soon, it wouldn't matter who was sending the assassins, or whether King Asperion bothered to pursue them. Sylvan and Thorne had a plan—one that would free them from the necessity of currying favor with anyone but themselves.

More importantly, their plan would free the humans and return control of the Vales to their hands.

The sunset had faded into twilight purple light that washed down the tower steps like a waterfall as Sylvan and Thorne descended. It felt altogether too peaceful after the violence of the last few hours.

As the thought crossed his mind, a streak of pink light darted across his path, making him stop short. Before he could say as much, it was joined by a streak of bright green, and another of eye-searing orange.

"The shimmerlings are loose." Thorne crouched, reaching for a sky-blue lizard that was making its way up the wall. The little creature skittered away from him, tail wriggling. "How could that have happened?"

Sylvan had shut the cage himself, had slid the lock into place with his own hands. Just as he always did. "It couldn't," he said. "Someone set them free."

CHAPTER THREE

NEVE

The mage shoved Neve down the stairs and back to the first-floor hall, throwing her against the window like she was nothing more than a toy. His human victims paused their 'feasting' to watch, their expressions sleepy and half-lidded, as if they couldn't quite calculate what their reaction ought to be. To them, this scene would be occurring as if in a dream.

"Hungry, are you?" the mage asked, capturing her attention away from his pets. His straw-blond hair was plastered unevenly against his forehead as he loomed over her, his aura shifting at the edges the way auras always did when a mage performed magic.

Whatever spell he was attempting, it wouldn't work. Not on Neve. It had been that way since her birth, or so her mother had claimed. While the shimmerling relics had soothed the other babies to eerie silence in their cribs, Neve had wailed on well into the night until her mother had been forced to move them out of the village for fear of discovery.

Would that she'd remained hidden.

The woman mage in the green dress still lingered by the

stairs, but Neve couldn't see past the blond mage to tell if she might be a source of assistance. Not likely, if she found coal-eating so very amusing.

The man grabbed Neve by the shoulders, giving her a shake that slammed her back against the wall. "I asked you a question, little hollow."

He was playing at being angry, the way someone keen to dole out punishments would play. She swallowed, recalling everything she'd taught herself about enthrallment. She had made it a lifelong study, out of necessity, and she knew well that the more enthralled a human was, the less nervous she should be.

It was difficult to stop her hands from shaking. Impossible.

"I must retrieve a basket of fruit," she said. "For... for my master."

Every human working in the fortress would have a master. They trailed after their mages or ran about on errands on their behalf, answering to 'hollow this' and 'hollow that.' The mage insult for humans. As though their powers filled the mages with anything worth having.

If power meant filling her soul with evil, Neve would much rather be hollow.

The mage leaned closer to her, and she had to force herself not to shrink away as he pressed his fingertips into her upper arms. "Perhaps you'll come to my rooms and entertain me."

No doubt he thought he was enthralling her with his poison-speaking powers. Not all the mages had those, but he'd demonstrated his abilities with his coal-swallowing pets. He probably even thought his magic could override that of her master's.

Every option that entered Neve's mind would land her in a dungeon, or worse. Knee to the groin? Dungeon. Stomp on those pretty shoes? Also dungeon. She realized she was trembling, but not from fear; no, it was rage that pulsed through her veins, tempting her to take catastrophic action she'd never be able to retract.

This was what humans in Vunmore endured on a daily basis. Their lives, their bodies, their very souls given to the control of others.

She could do nothing to help them.

"The basket," she said, forcing the words out from between clenched teeth. "For my master."

The mage lifted a finger, twisting a strand of her dark hair around it. And then he *pulled*. Pain sparked across her scalp, and she barely stopped herself from grimacing. If those humans were so enthralled that they could eat hot coals without protesting, she had to pretend not to feel the pain, either.

At what point would it be worth the high price to protest? Of revealing her immunity? When the tip of his knife cut into the softness of her throat?

"I saw you release those shimmerlings, little hollow," the mage said. "Did you do that for your master, too?" He stepped closer, bringing with him the sickening smell of sugar, mixed with blood. "What will he say, I wonder, when he finds you have dawdled in my bedchambers? Will he punish you? Or will he want to watch?"

If this mage forced her to his bedchambers, Neve would cut off his member and hang it on the front gate. Dungeon or no dungeon.

"Leave off, Evander." The woman mage's voice was bored, but there was an edge to it as well. As if forcing a hollow into his bed was where she drew the line. Hot coals were humorous, though. "She must be one of Sylvan's. They're never corruptible. His power's much too strong."

"All the more reason to play." Evander dragged her closer by that strand of hair, the pain stinging her scalp. "I'm not afraid of the bastard prince. Are you?"

She didn't reply.

But someone else did.

"Who is one of mine?"

Evander released her, stepping back so quickly that Neve would have laughed, had her body not been frozen in place by the sound of the newcomer's voice. Deep and resonant, with a confidence that dominated the hall even before she looked up and saw the man it belonged to.

Sylvan Everstone stood at the foot of the stairs, arms folded across his chest, the fading light casting half his body in shadow. He was taller than he'd seemed from the distant glimpses she'd caught during her tenure in the city, his dark red hair always making him easy to pick out. His body was slim and coiled with wiry muscle, his skin pale. The half of his face she could see was like a marble sculpture, his features carved in sharp lines. He was striking in a way that stole her breath.

And then he stepped into the light, revealing the slash of a scar that split the right side of his face. It began with a star of a prickle at his nose, then hooked around his cheekbone before cutting a diagonal path to his temple. It looked as if someone had tried to carve his flesh away. It looked as if they had very nearly succeeded.

No one knew how he'd come by that scar, at least among the humans. The prince had disappeared for three years; when he'd returned, he'd borne the mark.

If anything, it made him even more striking.

Evander was still close enough that Neve could see the way his hands shook before he pressed his fingertips into the small of his back to stop the trembling. There was no way that Sylvan had not heard Evander call him a 'bastard prince.'

"Your Highness." Even with his hands shaking, Evander's bow was a shallow one. Neve would not have risked such a slight.

The prince stepped closer, elbowing Evander casually out of

the way as his attention landed on Neve. His eyes were gray, like storm clouds hanging above a landscape of winter white.

She didn't know why that surprised her.

"One of mine," he repeated. "This one?"

Out of the corner of her eye, she saw Evander nod, throat bobbing as he swallowed his fear.

But Neve had her own fear to consider. She pressed her tongue to the roof of her mouth, gritting her teeth against the urge to run. To escape this man who was studying her the way a predator might study its prey. He must have dozens of servants. Hundreds. If he recognized her lie, the dungeons would be the best she could hope for.

If he recognized her lie, he would cut her apart. Piece by piece.

The prince scanned her face as if she were a mystery he intended to pick apart, thread by thread, until he unraveled her every last secret. He wasn't even touching her, yet she could feel his nearness, as if his aura were threaded with lightning. His closeness made her hair want to stand on end.

This was a man who scrutinized every detail with deep intensity. This was a man who would remember the face of every single servant he'd ever enthralled.

Neve's knees trembled, threatening to dump her on the floor at his feet.

"One of mine," he said again. "Yes. She is."

Neve blinked, lips parting in surprise before she had the sense to snap them back together. The Soulslayer was claiming her as his? *Why?*

Probably for the same reasons Evander had wanted to claim her.

The woman mage dropped into a curtsy, much deeper than her friend's. "Apologies, Your Highness. We hadn't seen her before."

Though she had been the one to suggest Sylvan's ownership

in the first place. Not that Neve planned to say so. She planned to say nothing at all, in fact. If these mages wanted to play out some little drama with her as the pawn, she'd let it happen. And she'd take her first chance to abandon the board.

She didn't know why the prince was choosing to claim her, but it would not be to her benefit. The tales of the Soulslayer's cruelty ran deep, and she did not doubt that this intervention would come with a price.

As Evander's friend curtseyed low, her green skirts pooling around her knees, Evander seemed to remember his spine. He straightened, squaring his shoulders. "So it was you who ordered her to release the lizards then? Your Highness?"

A challenge. Sylvan's eyes snapped back to Neve's, holding her gaze for a beat. Two. Had she not known better—had it not been absolutely impossible—she would have sworn the spark in his eyes seemed almost... amused?

But no. He would punish her for her impudence. He may believe her to be in thrall, but he must know that she wasn't one of his human servants. Even if he had too many to remember all their faces—and she had trouble believing that sharp gaze missed much of anything—he would never have instructed her to release the shimmerlings.

"Pathetic creatures," he said, eyes still drilling into hers. "I need better than that inferior crop. Of course I told her to release them."

With that, he took her by the arm, fingers hooking beneath her elbow more gently than she would have expected as he tugged her away from the wall.

For the first time, she noticed Prince Thorne standing on the bottom step behind Sylvan. Had he witnessed the entire interaction? There was no way to tell as he stepped down from the tower stairs, eyes on Evander's forgotten human pets. He clearly intended to linger. No doubt he would continue their torture, or concoct one of his own.

Neve had no opportunity to discover which it would be as Sylvan pulled her down the corridor and away from his fellow mages. Neve caught a flash of blue as a straggling shimmerling darted through a crack in the wall.

"Interesting choice," Prince Sylvan murmured, his voice little more than a rumble beside her ear. "Did another mage bid you release the lizards? If so, I would know who."

Neve swallowed, aware of the need to tread with care. He had not *commanded* her to speak, yet a human in his thrall would likely answer the question without hesitation. She might try to lie, but Evander could not have instructed her to release the shimmerlings, and she did not know any other mages' names.

If Prince Sylvan caught her in a lie, she would not last the night. There was no doubt in her mind that he was trying to use his magic on her now, though she could make out no shift in his aura. Perhaps he'd learned to hide the signs.

As that thought crossed her mind, another more sinister one followed: for who was to say *his* magic would not work on her, even if the other mages' did not? He was Prince Sylvan Everstone, the Soulslayer. Who knew what he could do?

The corridor ended abruptly in a stone archway, with no door to separate the grounds from the interior fortress. Even through the depths of winter, the mages' roses bloomed, and the castle remained warm and comfortable.

Sylvan's hand was warm on her wrist, his aura golden as he led her out into the garden. "I dislike the practice, myself," he said. Neve's expression must have shown her confusion, because he added, "Of making relics of the shimmerlings."

"But you do it." Neve spoke without thinking, wishing she could snatch the words back as soon as they'd been spoken. "You kill them. You enchant them."

The prince would stop her now. He would force her to eat a poisonous weed. He would slip a knife between her ribs. Or he would shove her against the nearest tree and—

"I do what I must," Sylvan said softly.

He led her through the garden, the foliage thickening until she was moving branches out of the way to keep them from hitting her face, until the path petered into stepping stones, and then nothing at all. She felt sure that he would stop at any moment, that he would finish what Evander had wanted to start.

But the Soulslayer kept going.

When they reached the outer wall, he grabbed a bunch of hanging ivy and pulled it aside.

A door. There was a *door* back here. And he was offering her passage through it. She hesitated, trying to discern what trap he might be leading her to. What sort of horrors might lay beyond it.

It looked like a regular door. Like iron set within a wall of stone.

Sylvan paused, still holding on to her arm. "You may come work for me. If you like."

He offered it like a prize, instead of the prison sentence it was. Did he truly believe she would accept that? Neve wrenched her hand out of his grasp. "So you can force me to eat coals?"

Not an enthralled human's response. But then, an enthralled human wouldn't have asked about the shimmerlings, either. The shield of the ruse was gone, if it had ever existed at all.

The prince's expression didn't change. He might have been made of stone, except for the spots of red that flickered quickly through his aura. She wondered if he knew he was giving himself away. "I will see that you are not harmed," he said.

She didn't believe him. She couldn't. She pointed to the door. Surely he hadn't led her here just to taunt her. Even if he had, he would quickly learn that she was fast, that she would escape him before he could blink. They were at the wall now; she could climb the ivy. Scale a tree. Be gone, as quick as the shimmerlings.

"May I go?" she asked.

He clenched his fists, then flattened his hands against his sides briefly before settling on folding his arms across his chest. "I am no captor."

Neve didn't hesitate. She threw herself at the door, her shoulder hitting the iron as she tried to shove it open. He was taunting her, still dangling the possibility of escape. He would snatch it away. He would have a key around his neck, and she'd have to kill him if she wanted to retrieve it. He would force her to do unspeakable things, keep her in his dungeon. Panic clawed up her throat as if desperate to be freed from the cage of her chest, turning each breath into a ragged gasp in the near silence of the garden.

A tendril of magic sparkled out from Sylvan Everstone's aura, and the latch clicked.

Neve pushed the door open. And then, she ran.

CHAPTER FOUR

SYLVAN

$\mathcal{B}$y the time Sylvan returned to the main part of the fortress, the gardens were alight with fleeing shimmerlings. Too fast for the mages and human servants who'd arrived to chase them down, they streaked through the foliage like oversized sparks.

That human woman, whoever she was, may well have reintroduced the creatures into the wild. A species native to the Vales, they'd been bred in captivity for centuries by power-hungry mages like himself.

The shimmerlings were of no importance. The mages kept them in abundance. If Sylvan had his way, he'd have set them all free long ago.

The woman who *had* released them, however, was a riddle. Sylvan could still feel the press of her fingers against his sleeve, the savory scent of garden herbs cutting through the sweetness of lilies and festival pastries, and the hint of blood left after the interrogation. Making the day just a hint more bearable.

Her skin was a warm olive tone, with a splash of freckles dashed impertinently across her nose. Her eyes, a bolt of green beneath the fringe of chestnut hair, had flashed with defiance.

And rather than tamping it down, as nearly any other human or mage would have done in his presence, she'd let that defiance fly.

Sylvan had released her thrall the moment he'd seen her trapped in Evander's sneering gaze, and she'd used that freedom to challenge him outright, throwing insults and veiled accusations in his face. A rarity indeed.

Perhaps he should have allowed her to remain in thrall long enough to tell him the identity of her true master, the one who'd bade her release the shimmerlings. The very idea of keeping anyone under thrall made Sylvan's throat burn with bile. No, he'd rather wonder at it forever than make use of such an abhorrent magic—though someone *must* have commanded it of her. A human wouldn't have risked such a thing on her own, unless she were under a mage's control.

Though he could not help but think that *this* human might.

It would be easy enough to discover her identity, to have her followed through the city and find where she laid her head at night. Even now, it was not too late. She couldn't have gotten far.

Again, it would be the wise course of action. The mage who'd enthralled her to release the shimmerlings might have been playing a prank—but they also might be a rival. It would be well to discover their identity.

Sylvan would not have minded seeing those eyes again, either.

But no. Best to let her go. If another mage wished to challenge him, they'd show themselves soon enough. With such petty attempts at sabotage, they could not be much of a threat in any case.

Thorne was waiting for him when he reached the fortress, one shoulder propped against a column, his arms and legs crossed in a show of nonchalance. When Sylvan joined him, he straightened, arranging a look of surprise across his features.

"Brother," he said. "Forgive me, but could that be *amusement* on your face?"

Sylvan crossed his arms, mimicking Thorne's stance. "And should I not be amused?"

Thorne grinned, no doubt charmed by his own hilarity, and shook a lock of sun-kissed hair out of his eyes. "Perhaps I must define the emotion for you, brother. It concerns a state of gentle mirth, you see. Both of those things being most foreign to you indeed."

Should any other mage speak to Sylvan that way—the king excepted, he supposed—he would hang them from one of the balconies until they wept with regret. Even with Thorne, it could sometimes be a near thing.

But Sylvan still imagined he could smell a hint of rosemary on the air. "I assure you I am acquainted with the feeling of mirth."

Thorne raised a finger. "But not gentleness."

An iridescent shimmerling skittered over the toe of Sylvan's shoe. "Perhaps not."

Thorne straightened, pressing the back of his hand against Sylvan's forehead. "No fever. Still, I ought to call for a physician. You sound altogether too calm. Perhaps you've been replaced by an imposter Sylvan. A spirit, come to lure me into the abyss."

"The only place I shall lure you is into silence."

"But you've forgotten, brother. We have a ball to attend."

Oh, that Sylvan could have forgotten. He'd done what he could to set it out of his mind, but it was full dark now, and even King Asperion, in all his absentmindedness, would miss them if they stayed away.

A room full of smug, gossiping strangers who were only polite because their fear of him outweighed their contempt—by a sliver of a margin—was not the way he wanted to spend an evening. Preferably ever.

"It wouldn't be so bad if the decor were a bit more cheerful," Thorne was saying. "When I am king..."

But Sylvan didn't hear what his brother would do when he became king. As he spoke, a thread of smoke wafted around the corner, and Sylvan froze as it was followed by the monstrous form of a wraith. Its smoke-wreathed horns nearly scraped the ceiling, its eyes red as sundown, and it filled the corridor behind Thorne with unrestrained menace.

Blood beat a rhythm in Sylvan's ears, thick and disorienting, and the hallway tilted as fear rose in his gut as if to choke him.

The only way to overcome a wraith was through quick and decisive action. And he'd already hesitated too long.

Move. He had to *move*.

Sylvan shoved Thorne aside, fingertips tingling as he readied a stream of magefire. How the beast had breached the barrier to arrive here from the Miragelands, he did not know. But he wouldn't allow it to murder his brother and wreak havoc on the city.

A hand landed on his shoulder. "Easy, brother." Thorne's voice was muffled behind the war-drum call of Sylvan's pulse, the crackle of waiting magefire seething in his skin. "It is only sugar."

Sylvan shook his head, not understanding. The corridor had narrowed to a tunnel, those red eyes the only thing he could see. He could not find his voice to tell his brother to run. Thorne might have met with wraiths, but he hadn't lived alongside them. He'd never felt the depths of their claws sinking into his flesh. And Sylvan intended to keep it that way.

But Thorne stepped forward and broke a spine from the wraith's back, then bit it in half. "A sculpture, brother. For the ball."

Air rushed into Sylvan's lungs, mixed with the smell of sugar and candied fruit. He blinked, jerking his gaze to the floor. The beast had been mounted atop a cart, though the servant who'd been pushing it must have fled.

Thorne swiped a hand through the demon-wreathing smoke, twisting a curl of spun sugar around his forefinger. "Quite realistic."

For once, there was no jest in his voice. But the solemn line of his mouth and the worried tilt of his head were much worse. Sylvan would rather have his derision than his concern.

He fumbled into his jacket pocket for his gloves and pulled them on, hoping to dampen the unshed static of his magefire. "I shall impale the chef on his own knife."

Thorne's expression lightened. He was nothing if not easy to redirect. "Alas, brother. I fear that would make us late."

—✳—

KING ASPERION HAD CHOSEN to drown his ballroom in shades of black and red. Crimson streamers slithered from the ceiling like waterfalls of blood, and the floor was concealed beneath a shroud of billowing fog which, though it rose no higher than Sylvan's knees, gave him the disorienting impression that he was walking on uneven ground.

Thorne snatched a glass of wine from a passing tray. "Explains the wraith sculpture, at least."

Indeed, similar sculptures rose from the mist at every turn, horns and jagged wings spearing toward the ceilings. Even knowing that they were fakes, Sylvan had to suppress a shudder.

If the other guests found the decor off-putting, they didn't show it. The floor was already crowded with dancers, bodies pressed so tight they could hardly be said to be dancing at all. Other guests lounged at tables or settees, picking at the mountains of refreshments. One mage, a gray-haired lord Sylvan had only ever seen in passing, had taken up a spot at the pedestal of one of the monsters, where he leaned back into the shell of its wing.

"I don't know why they want to experience the Miragelands before they're forced to go there," Sylvan said. "There are still ten days left."

Sylvan might be the only one who'd survived three years in the place, but every mage over the age of twelve made the Return. Every three years, without fail. They'd all seen it, survived it—the wraiths, the ruins, the harshness of the sky. What a theme for a ball.

"They're whistling in the dark, brother," Thorne replied. "That's all. No one likes the Return."

"They do have the option of forgoing it entirely."

Thorne twirled his wine glass between two fingers. "And sacrifice their powers? You're dreaming. I do like that optimism from you, though. Truly refreshing. Now, I wonder where the king is. I'd love for him to see me so I can get the fuck out of here."

Sylvan followed his brother's gaze across the room. He didn't see King Asperion. But someone else did catch his eye.

Evander stood beside a fountain of red and black punch, his hair plastered to his head like a helmet. He was speaking to Fern, who was looking around the ballroom as if she expected someone to accost them at any moment. Whatever they were discussing, she didn't seem to want to be doing it in public.

All Sylvan could see was the way Evander had twisted the human woman's hair around his finger, the way he'd smiled as he caused her pain. As he caused her fear. Enthralled or not, her fear had been patently obvious.

And then there was the matter of the humans he'd been torturing. Even among the mages, that level of cruelty was... uncommon. And they called *him* a monster.

Thorne had sent the humans away to be healed. And Sylvan

could comfort himself with the fact that this world would soon belong to their kind once again.

They just had to hold out until the Return.

Evander's gaze snagged on Sylvan's, and he straightened. Sylvan held his gaze until the other man flushed and looked away.

Sylvan didn't like it. He didn't like it at all. On the heels of an assassination attempt on Thorne, the man's behavior was suspicious, at best. Treacherous at worst.

"Ah," said Thorne. "Here he comes now."

For a moment, Sylvan thought Thorne meant Evander. But then he saw the king, ambling toward them with one hand lifted in greeting. Asperion wore a golden yellow coat, with bright purple buttons, a waterfall of tassels dripping from each sleeve. His golden hair was a tangled mess, his bald spot reflecting a shining circle of red light on the back of his skull. One of his bootlaces trailed behind him, making every step a risk. Which would have been far less alarming had he not been carrying a fat clay cask, so large that Sylvan feared he would drop the thing and shatter it all over the floor. Especially given the way he bumbled through the ballroom, tripping every few steps. Surely he wasn't *drinking* out of the thing.

Ridiculous as he was, the guests parted around the king as though he were using his legendary poison-speech abilities on them. Asperion was particularly strong in the power, personally holding the majority of the humans in this realm in thrall by imbuing his powers into the relics that Sylvan created.

Interestingly, poison-speech had no effect on mages. Sylvan often wondered if poison-speakers had been considered powerless before they'd invaded the Vales. He'd never been able to parse out a different use for the power while in the Miragelands.

Thorne, who'd somehow collected a woman while Sylvan

was distracted by Evander, let out a small sigh. "All hail the king," he muttered.

Asperion threw one arm over Sylvan's shoulder, bringing with him a wave of spicy cologne and stale tobacco. Sylvan sniffed, wondering if there were any known power that could help him restrain a sneeze.

Thorne grinned, clearing his throat, though he might as well have thrown his head back and laughed. At least someone found the king's antics to be hilarious. Thorne's date had draped herself against his body, as sinuous as the decor, and Sylvan had no doubt they'd be absenting themselves as soon as possible.

"The party is a success!" Asperion released Sylvan at last so he could throw his free hand toward the ceiling. He was still cradling that obscenely large cask, no doubt for reasons he'd soon unveil to them in a slew of nonsensical detail. "Hear the music? I had the players brought in from Riles. Across the sea. I thought they'd be quaint, perhaps a bit of a laugh, but they're actually rather charming. Are they not?"

"Fabulous, Father," Thorne said, though he was looking at his date like she was the dessert course and he intended to skip to the end of the meal. "You've outdone yourself."

Asperion waved him away, snorting a laugh. Gods, but Sylvan hated that laugh. "Nonsense, nonsense. A bit of direction here and there. That was my only contribution. Now, boys, if you'll indulge me. I'd hoped to discuss a project I've been working on."

Across the room, Evander broke away from his conversation with Fern. And then, to Sylvan's surprise, he started to make his way toward them.

"More science, Father?" Thorne asked.

Asperion chuckled again. Like a piglet digging its nose in a trough. "You know me and my little projects. Must keep busy somehow."

As if ruling a kingdom, or three, were not enough.

Evander joined them and sketched a bow to the king, which Asperion didn't even appear to see. His eyes were alight with whatever nonsense he was spouting to Thorne, whose expression was open with interest—though his hand, Sylvan noted, drifted lower on his date's back by the moment.

Evander stopped beside Sylvan, dragging his tongue along his upper lip like a snake sniffing for prey. "It's funny, Soulslayer. But I've never seen that hollow woman before. Not in the castle, and certainly not with you."

Either the alcohol was making him bolder, or he'd spent the afternoon rehearsing that little speech in the mirror so he could make a better showing. When Sylvan had interrupted him with the pretty human woman earlier, he'd looked frightened enough to piss his pants. Was that why he'd made a point of joining them now? To prove Sylvan didn't frighten him?

Not many people dared use the name 'Soulslayer' to his face.

"There are a lot of hollows," Sylvan said, doing his best to channel Thorne's talent for sounding bored.

"You don't have very many though, do you?" Evander sipped his drink, as if they were discussing the weather. "Just that old git with the spectacles, yes?"

"Stay away from her," Sylvan said mildly. "Or I will need to slit your throat and hang you from the balustrades by your toes. I wonder how large a puddle your blood will make. Hm?"

He shouldn't betray so much. Demons, he usually didn't. But the thought of Evander touching a woman, any woman, and forcing her to see to his pleasures—it stoked the anger in Sylvan's chest, burning holes in his carefully constructed walls.

Evander's eyes flashed, and he opened his mouth to respond. Before he could spill whatever ill-considered threat or insult he had planned, Asperion stepped between them.

The king held the clay cask out in front of him with both hands, nodding at Sylvan and Evander expectantly.

"What's this?" Sylvan asked, barely managing to smooth the

irritation out of his tone, and only at the last moment. What the fuck was wrong with him tonight? If he kept this up, he would destroy everything he and Thorne had been working for.

Thorne withdrew his tongue from his date's ear to say, "It's a secret, apparently."

"Come now, I promise you'll see." Asperion winked. "But first, the drop."

Thorne's date giggled and smacked him on the arm, then trotted over to the king. With a sly smile, she withdrew the bottle-shaped pendant from around her neck. It was made of polished silver rather than glass, and it reflected the light in the ballroom in claw-like streaks. But Sylvan had no doubt that it held the same dollop of magepool water the rest of them carried.

While they watched, she unscrewed the cap and tipped the vial over Asperion's cask, allowing a single drop to run out.

Thorne gave her a wink, then withdrew his own vial and shook a drop into Asperion's cask. It was a wonder he didn't miss the cask entirely, with his attention locked on the sway of his date's hips as she strode away.

"That's my cue," Thorne said. "Behave yourselves, if you please."

Asperion chuckled and shook his head, as if nothing in the world could make him more proud.

And then he turned back to Sylvan and Evander. "Indulge me, won't you?"

Evander sketched another bow, then uncorked his vial and released a drop into the cask. Without so much as a glance at Sylvan, he strode away.

Dangerous, Sylvan thought. The man was dangerous. He ought to have Evander followed, to see what he was up to. And who he'd been meeting with. He acted like a cruel, indolent fool, but the abrupt change in his manner this evening was unnerving. It was entirely possible that he'd had something to do with the attempt on Thorne's life.

If Sylvan discovered that to be the case, it would not end well for Evander. He'd wish for his throat to be slit, before the end.

"Come, son." The king was practically shaking the cask at him, the water he'd already collected sloshing audibly against the sides.

I'm not your son, Sylvan thought. Keeping his eye on Evander, he unhooked his own vial from his waist and added a drop to Asperion's collection. No doubt the king was planning some kind of magepool-powered light show.

With a nod to the king, Sylvan turned on his heel and headed for the door.

"Come to my demonstration tomorrow," the king called after him. "It won't disappoint!"

It would, though. It always did. Pretending he hadn't heard, Sylvan slipped away into the crowd.

CHAPTER FIVE

NEVE

*A*fter the stifling confines of the fortress, escaping into the city felt like pulling in a lungful of air after hours of swimming underwater. The streets were quiet, if not deserted, the festival decorations mercifully fewer than they'd been inside the castle. Banners drooped between rooftops, blacking out swaths of night sky, and mage-lit candles flared on every available ledge.

Neve could almost pretend the humans had chosen to decorate the streets themselves. That the festival would be an actual celebration for them, that when the sun rose and illuminated the banners, their colors would portend a joyful celebration.

But true freedom could never happen among the mages.

Even if Sylvan Everstone had seen to her safety.

He was… not as she would have expected. Not that she'd ever anticipated she'd be walking the fortress halls with her arm in his. But if she had, she would not have predicted the strength of his muscles beneath her fingertips, nor the deliberate softness of his touch.

She would not have predicted that the man they called Soul-slayer would let her escape.

Or that, as she made her way through the streets like a shadow, her thoughts would be preoccupied by the cut of his cheekbones. No one called the Soulslayer handsome, at least not within her hearing. Not one person had ever mentioned the pale gray of his eyes, or the crooked character of his nose— broken at least once, if she was any judge.

No one called him handsome, yet he was inarguably so. The slash of a scar only enhanced the effect.

Foolish. Handsome or not, the Soulslayer was likely following her now, or sending one of his lackeys to see to it. He would drag her back to the fortress. Interrogate her for releasing his shimmerlings. He would make her his servant until he tired of her, or forgot about her.

And here she was, thinking of the way the corner of his mouth had quirked, ever so slightly, when she'd challenged him.

He was Sylvan Everstone. Not some man she'd met in a tavern.

She quickened her steps, eager to return to the garret she rented on the outskirts of town. She'd failed in her request to retrieve a shimmerling for Lydia, but she could wait no longer. Tomorrow, she'd quit Vunmore and head for the coast. Perhaps she could barter passage to Etra by offering to scrub decks or wash dishes.

If all else failed, she'd make an excellent stowaway.

Near the fortress, the streets were wide, smelling of pine buildings and woodsmoke and baking bread. As she came down the hill, however, the streets grew narrower, the buildings more slanted, until they began to resemble drunken friends leaning upon one another after taking too much wine.

There was still an undercurrent of baked bread in the air, but it was buried, unfortunately, beneath layers of grease, boiled vegetables, and refuse left too long in the bin. And, of course, as she slipped into the alley she called home, the unmistakable sting of piss.

At this point, she didn't care. All she wanted was to sneak up to her attic corner—which she'd begged the landlord to rent her for mere pennies—and snuggle into the pile of rugs and blankets she called a bed.

Well, maybe not *all* she wanted. She could have done with a mug of ale. But it had been a long night. Best to head straight home.

Something flickered in the darkness ahead and she paused, slipping back into the depths of the shadows. It might be a street cat, prowling for a morsel. And yet somehow, she knew it was not.

Her eyes were sharpened for the darkness after her trek through the city, which was why she was able to make out the shape of a person. They might have been waiting for anyone, for anything. They might have descended from their bed to smoke a roll of cloves, or stopped in the alley to respond to nature's call on the way home from a public house.

But there was no telltale flare of a cigarette, no splash of urine against stone. The person did not move.

She couldn't see their face—only the long line of the nose in profile, the heavyset hulk of the shoulders—yet she knew why they were here. They were watching her door.

Perhaps the Soulslayer had not let her go so easily after all.

Mourning the loss of her blankets, she slid deeper into the shadows, moving soundlessly out of the alley. She had not told Sylvan her name, had given no hint of where she lived. But he was a prince, and a powerful mage. If he wished to find her, he could.

She was not without her own talents, however. He wouldn't find her an easy quarry.

Neve carved a jagged path back through the city, circling

around several times to check whether she'd been followed. She didn't make her way all the way to the fortress, instead cutting over to the eastern side of the hill and, when she was certain that she was still alone, to a shop with teacups painted on the glass windows and a white-painted sign declaring Tea & Tinctures.

Neve was not fool enough to approach the front door. She went to the back instead and rapped a quiet rhythm, hoping Lydia was not too deeply asleep—or too deeply enthralled—to hear.

The door opened so quickly, the apothecary must already have been awake. She frowned into the gap, clearly ready to scold whatever stranger had appeared at her door in the middle of the night. When she lifted her candle so she could make out Neve's face, however, her eyes widened.

She opened the door, ushering Neve inside. "Will your nighttime escapades never cease, girl?"

Neve shut the door behind her, drawing the curtain to hide the light as Lydia lit a lantern. She was still tsking and clucking her tongue, even as she set a kettle on the already-burning fire.

Gray-haired and amply shaped, Lydia was a first-rate apothecary and enthusiast of hot drinks in all forms. Mostly mint tea, since the plant grew in abundance, but she grew all manner of herbs in her rooftop garden, coaxing remedies and drinks out of every one. This evening, her hair was swept into a messy bun, her feet bare as she padded around the kitchen.

Lydia uncorked a jar of tea leaves and shook some into the kettle. Neve didn't know what kind they were—she couldn't tell the difference—but Lydia always insisted that there were teas for illness and teas for sadness, teas for wedding days and teas for funerals.

Neve supposed she'd be getting a tea for exhausted, uninvited guests.

"What are you doing here, girl?" Lydia asked. "There's no deliveries this week. You know that."

Neve did know. It was one of the reasons she'd chosen to disappear now, rather than after the festival. It was a small reason, one to add to the massive benefit of the mages locking themselves in their fortress for a week—which they would do after the festival ended, for famously unknown reasons—but it was still a reason.

Lydia often called upon Neve to run deliveries, though she scarcely needed to. Given the popularity of her shop, she could rely on the people to come to her. But Neve was grateful for the job. She didn't have any friends. She didn't have any family. Lydia was not her mother—could not be anything like her mother, because she didn't know Neve's secret—but she was the closest thing to a friend Neve could let herself have.

As Lydia set a flawless teacup on the table, though, Neve couldn't let herself forget the bouquet of shimmerling bones tied together with a ribbon and mounted above the door she'd just entered. She couldn't let herself forget that, like every other human in the Vales, Lydia was enthralled.

It had been foolish to come here.

"Drink," Lydia commanded, and Neve obeyed, though the tea was bitter on her tongue. "What happened? Your young man toss you out on your ear?"

Neve snorted. "I don't have a young man."

"Your young woman, then."

"Don't have one of those, either."

Lydia wrapped her hands around her own mug of tea, studying Neve like she was a riddle in need of solving. "You charge too little for your services."

Neve blinked, confused. "What does that have to do with—"

"You'll stay here," Lydia interrupted, "in my spare room. You'll continue to deliver for me, and you'll earn the usual rate."

Emotion choked Neve's throat, Lydia's kindness too much to

absorb. She shook her head. And before she could think better of it, she spoke the truth. "I can't. I'm sailing for Etra this week."

Lydia scoffed. "Poor teas in Etra."

Neve laughed, the sound emerging like half a sob. Lydia put a hand over hers. "Whatever happened, child, we'll make it right. You're not alone."

But Neve was alone. She was more alone than any human had ever been. For years, she'd held out hope, believing that she couldn't possibly be the only human capable of resisting the mages' thrall, and she'd searched. With every town she visited, every village she passed through, every stranger she encountered, she'd searched for someone else like herself. But she'd only ever come up empty.

With Lydia's hand on hers, her sharp gaze softened in concern, Neve could almost believe the apothecary was right. She could almost believe she mattered to Lydia.

And the mages kept this woman—this cranky, brilliant, kind woman—from ever being her full self. They kept her in chains.

All the feelings she'd been trying to tamp down since setting foot in the fortress this afternoon came boiling to the surface in one wretched tide of feeling. Humans didn't deserve to live this way. The woman in the fortress with the four baskets. The humans forced to devour hot coals, who would likely be dealing with the aftermath of the injuries for the rest of their lives.

Neve pulled her hand from Lydia's and stood. Before she could think better of it, she swiped the bouquet of shimmerling bones from their hook above the door. Hands shaking, she snapped the bones in half.

Lydia blinked, startled. "What…"

But Neve was already shaking her head, regret turning a sickly spiral in her stomach.

Lydia rose from her seat, eyes clearing, and folded Neve into a sudden hug. "Reckless child," she said softly. "What have you done?"

Neve wanted to return the embrace, but Lydia was already releasing her. She hurried for the nearest cabinet, throwing the door open and removing a burlap sack.

"We will need to get you out." She slid a loaf of bread into the bag, followed by a handful of apples from the back of the cabinet. She must have been saving those. "A blanket, too. It's cold in the forest. Etra, you said? You may have difficulty getting out now."

Neve stood motionless by the door, gripping the bones. They felt so delicate between her fingers. So fragile. Was it truly this easy to break such an enchantment?

Lydia was still talking, the sack now bulging as she set it on the table. "Why would you do that? How *could* you do it?"

She shouldn't have been able to. Not with the thrall bathing Lydia's home, her shop, in its power. "I just…" She trailed off, licking her lips. "The thrall…"

But she couldn't explain it to Lydia. She couldn't make the words come out, could not confirm the secret, even if Lydia deserved to know it. Even if she'd already guessed. When others knew of Neve's immunity, it put them in danger.

When others knew of her immunity, they used her.

Lydia paused in her preparations long enough to give Neve's shoulder a brief squeeze. "It was a mistake. That's all."

But she did not say the mages would take mercy on her. She did not say it was defensible, or even understandable. The mages wouldn't see it that way.

And they would be coming.

Lydia cinched the bag shut and slid it toward her. "Follow the road across the plains until you reach the southern woodlands. But stay concealed. With any luck, they'll be too busy with their festival to notice one missing relic."

Neve swallowed, throat dry. "What about you?"

"Shimmerling bones are easy enough to replace." There was bitterness in her tone, but she gave Neve a small smile.

47

If she guessed what had happened, what Neve was, she did not say.

The shop door burst open, its glass panels cracking as it slammed into the wall, and then the shop was filled with black-uniformed poison-speakers. Display tables crashed to the ground as they elbowed their way through, filling the air with the scent of mint and black tea.

The first poison-speaker to reach them took Lydia by the wrist, his aura swimming. "Your relic is broken." He wrenched her away from the table, and she stumbled, held up only by the strength of his grip.

Neve stepped around the table, trying to shield Lydia with her body. Not easy, when he was already holding onto her. "It was me. I broke the bones."

"Hush, girl," Lydia hissed.

But Neve wouldn't. She'd save her friend, if she could.

If the poison-speaker put Lydia under thrall and demanded the truth, she would tell it. She'd have no choice.

"I was dusting a cobweb from the wall," Neve said. "I knocked the bones down and stepped on them by accident. It wasn't my mistress's fault. She fired me. Kicked me out. She—"

"Enough." The poison-speaker glared at her, and she snapped her mouth shut. She had the distinct impression that he did not want to be here. Perhaps she'd interrupted his dice game or extended his shift. Perhaps he'd been halfway to his favorite whorehouse and forced to turn around.

She'd been a fool to think she could save Lydia. She had, if anything, doomed them both.

The poison-speaker gave Lydia a shove, releasing her wrist, and she fell to the floor, knocking her head against the wall. "Re-enthrall her," he said.

For a moment, Neve thought he would buy the story and let them both go. But then he grabbed her wrist and wrenched her hands behind her back, smirking when she grunted in pain.

Because it didn't matter if he bought the story or not. Destruction of relics meant the dungeon. Simple as that.

Neve tried to look back, to see if Lydia would stir or if the hit to her head had rendered her unconscious. But the poison-speakers clustered around her, blocking her view, and Lydia was lost behind a wall of black uniforms as they wrenched Neve out into the street.

CHAPTER SIX

SYLVAN

*S*ylvan nearly forgot about the demonstration.

He'd spent half the night lying awake and staring at the ceiling, trying to stop his racing thoughts from gaining weight as they tumbled around his skull. So it wasn't until the clatter of arriving courtiers crescendoed to a roar outside his chamber window that he recalled the king's invitation.

Asperion fancied himself a scholar. He spent more time tinkering with magic in his so-called laboratory than he did governing his nation. Pushing the boundaries of magic, he claimed, though Sylvan had never seen him produce anything more potent than a particularly pretty firework.

By the time Sylvan staggered out of his rooms, the halls were empty. Not even the human servants remained.

The courtyard was packed with mages when he entered, ignoring their bows—too shallow for true courtesy, but deep enough to betray their fear—to join Thorne at the front. At least this morning's decorations weren't as dour as last night's. Colorful flower garlands hung from the balconies and candles had been set into every alcove. Sylvan would probably be called upon later to light them with magefire. Even if a match would do perfectly well.

There *were* more of the sugar sculptures arranged in the courtyard, but in the sunlight, their true nature was obvious. Not a threat, but a delicacy. Leave it to Asperion to cast the most horrible dangers of the Miragelands in sugar. He who would enter those lands surrounded by bodyguards, the wraiths no threat to him at all.

Despite the emptiness of the fortress's halls, there were no humans in sight here, either. It felt strange for there to be no servants moving among the crowd to offer refreshments or assistance. Humans were always easily distinguished, their clothing drab in comparison to the garish excess of his fellow mages. Sylvan glanced up at the balconies, but they, too, were packed with mages. Faces he knew. Faces he despised. And, somewhat surprisingly, a fair few faces he didn't recognize.

Like Sylvan, Evander had found a spot near the front of the crowd. He smirked when their eyes met, and the glint in his said he hadn't forgotten their conversation from last night. Or the threat he'd prodded Sylvan into making.

Dangerous, indeed.

"The king must have invited every mage in the city," Sylvan commented, as much to distract himself from Evander than because he wanted conversation.

"Not only the city." Thorne hitched his chin toward the gate, where a pair of their allies stood with their backs to the wall. Jessa and Kael were rarely in Vunmore, instead favoring their woodland estate in the south. It was a lovely spot, not far from the sea. Their presence here was a surprise, truly. Apparently, this demonstration was to be one for the entire country to witness. Everyone the king could summon.

"That explains all the strangers," Sylvan said.

"Indeed."

Sylvan looked at his brother. Thorne seemed to be struggling to maintain his typical air of casual disinterest, an uncharacteristic crease parting the center of his brow. He was running the tip of his thumb back and forth along the hem of his shirt, unable to fully suppress his nerves.

Sylvan was about to ask what could be setting him off balance today, with a list of possibilities including the excess of drink and the exertions required of him by the woman he'd been with last night.

The quip dried on his lips as King Asperion came into focus.

The king stood in the limited open space that remained in the courtyard, next to a line of freshly painted red circles. He wore a golden circlet, one with thin bands of intertwining gold. Not a crown he typically wore to greet his subjects, but a crown he wore for action.

A crown he wore for the hunt.

But it was his demeanor, his bearing, that twisted a knot in Sylvan's stomach.

The king looked… well, sober. Every button in place, every bootlace secured, his feet planted steadily in the courtyard. No evidence of drink, no sign of a hangover. Though he gave Sylvan a smile when their eyes met, it did not reach his eyes.

Gone was the man who'd slung his arm around Sylvan's shoulder, who'd flirted with Thorne's date.

In his place stood a new man entirely.

This man, the smile said, would not be so easily dismissed.

"Well met, Prince Sylvan," Asperion said. So much for 'my son.' Sylvan could only bow in response, unsure yet of how this would need to be played. "Are you ready to see what I've been preparing?"

Sylvan kept his expression carefully neutral. "Always, King Asperion."

Asperion turned, making it clear that he meant to address the entire assembly. "Even as we celebrate the Return," he said, "I know how much we also dread it. That we must endure the brutality of the Miragelands in order to maintain our powers has been a plague on our people for generations."

Sylvan clenched his fists by his sides. These people had only ever scratched the surface of that brutality. They didn't know the terror of waking alone to a circling cloud of wraiths, the ground slithering beneath your head. The days leaking away without rest as predators stalked you across a barren landscape.

They did not know how the place could cleave a soul in half.

Asperion bent. And retrieved the cask he'd filled with their magepool drops last night.

Cold dread unspooled in Sylvan's gut.

"I will go alone to the Miragelands," Asperion announced. "I will infuse new magic into the drops of magepool water you so generously entrusted to me. And your magic will be restored."

It took a moment for the people to absorb what their king had said. They, too, were used to light shows and nonsense. They, too, had expected absurdity.

And then, their faces shifted. From furrowed brows and tilted heads to open-mouthed delight that had them rising onto their toes. Eager. Hungry.

Their nightmares would have been fueled by memories of the Miragelands, their anxieties building as the day of the Return grew ever closer. They might lounge in the shadows of wraith sculptures, might dance and writhe and fuck under decorations that pretended to make light of the lands they all feared, but no one wanted to go back there. Not one of them.

"Brilliant, Father." Thorne's tone was careful. Not quite impassive, yet not quite enthusiastic, either. All their plans were crumbling, and he couldn't quite hide his dismay. Though no one but Sylvan would know the reason for it. "Amazing. Only... your poison-speech enthralls the majority of the hu—the hollow population. Will it hold? With you away in the Miragelands?"

Murmurs broke out among the crowd, the hopeful light

dimming out of the mages' eyes as they realized that Thorne had a point. There were many more humans than there were mages—many—and the mages' powers had dimmed over the past three years. They weren't prepared to handle even a hint of unrest.

Asperion's smile widened, as if he'd been awaiting this very question. Still clutching the cask, he turned a slow circle, and the crowd quieted. Instead of addressing them, though, Asperion said, "Bring out the prisoners."

The ball of dread in Sylvan's stomach grew heavier.

The crowds moved aside as a gang of poison-speakers entered, their uniforms like ink stains spilled across a beautiful landscape. They flanked a group of bedraggled humans as if expecting a fight, but even with the guards blocking his line of sight, Sylvan could see that the humans walked with shoulders hunched, their ragged clothing fluttering around their legs. Even if they truly were criminals—doubtful, since humans were held in thrall—they posed no threat whatsoever.

When the lead poison-speaker stepped aside, Sylvan's breath caught in his throat.

The first human in the group was Flint.

The valet's eyes were glassed over with the telltale look of deep enthrallment. A tough kind of magic to hold, and not of much use unless you wanted someone to continue repeating the same task until the end of time.

It was a disgusting way to use magic. Though most mages would have argued it was more important to note that it was useless, as deeply enthralled humans had no autonomy at all and therefore made for frustrating servants.

To see the light in Flint's eyes dulled like that... it made Sylvan want to rip the entire fortress apart. Starting with the king.

He must have given a sign, a shuffle of his feet in Flint's direction, for Thorne lay a hand on his arm. "Steady, brother."

There was a warning in his eyes. And he wasn't wrong. Should Sylvan interfere, he'd be playing directly into Asperion's plans. The king had already proved unpredictable—and all too capable of deception.

"Step inside the circles," Asperion instructed.

The humans obeyed. Sylvan was aware that there were five, perhaps six other humans in the group, but he couldn't take his eyes from Flint. The valet had been perfectly well yesterday when he'd come to Thorne's rooms, when he'd helped to clear the aftermath of Sylvan's interrogation. What had happened between then and now? There was a dark bruise across the old man's cheek, and though he held his head straight, Sylvan had the distinct impression that it was a demand of the enthrallment; his muscles shook with the effort of it.

"In my absence," Asperion said, "the humans who plague our lands must not be permitted to take what is rightfully ours."

Sylvan choked back a snort, though there was truly no mirth in it. Not with Flint standing there, face ash gray. Rightfully theirs? These lands had been stolen, hand over fist.

With Thorne's help, and with the help of their allies, Sylvan intended to give them back.

The other courtiers, though, had no such compunctions. With the exception of Jessa and Kael, who stood together by the gate like statues, the courtiers jeered, calling out unintelligible words about the weakness and the evil of humans.

There was an undercurrent of hope in it, too. They didn't want to return to the Miragelands.

Whatever Asperion was about to do, they wanted it to work.

Asperion raised his hands, and the crowd quieted. "I have worked tirelessly over the last three years to develop this solution. I have personally studied and tested the bounds of magic as we know it. And I can stand before you today promising to take your place in the Miragelands, because I can promise your security in my absence."

He turned to the humans. "Stay within the circle," he said. "You are forbidden from moving."

A strange requirement. An enthralled person would not be likely to move in any case. But over time, when the mage who commanded them had gone, the magic would fade. Hence the shimmerling bones, the relics that kept them lethargic.

Most of the time, mages gave general commands. Decorate for the festival. Prepare a feast. Care for the horses. The humans would feel as if it was what they wished to do, as though it were the most important thing they might accomplish. But they could go about it their own way, provided that the mages had given room for them to do so. They could see to their own needs.

Certainly, mages like Evander abused the power. But it was not often done. Not out of a sense of mercy, but rather selfishness. Mages wanted to be served without question. That was the crux of it.

Asperion turned his back to the humans, who stood rigidly in their circles. Flint was trembling with the effort of standing still.

For a moment, Sylvan thought Asperion's gaze would fall on him. But it drifted instead to his right. To where Thorne stood. "You, son."

It was a summons, and Thorne recognized it as such. He stepped forward.

Asperion hitched his chin toward Flint. "Shove him."

Thorne blinked. "Sire?"

"Shove the valet," Asperion said. "He stands accused of attempting to murder you. Shove him out of his circle."

Sylvan's throat went dry. How had Asperion learned of the assassination attempt? How had he known of Flint's presence in the chamber?

The courtyard was too quiet as Thorne stepped forward, all the voices fallen silent. There was till the rustle of cloth, the shuffling of feet, but it felt as if their very breath had stilled in their throats. Thorne was gaping at Flint, eyes wide. So poor at hiding his emotions. So very poor.

He knew, as Sylvan did, that this was a trick. That when he pushed Flint out of that circle, something terrible would happen.

Sylvan felt himself move before he had quite decided he intended to do it. Whatever the king had planned, it was meant to punish him—it must be, as there was no way Asperion could be ignorant of the identity of his valet.

"I will do it," Sylvan said.

He did not look at the king, didn't want to know whether his eyes were flashing with anger or with smug satisfaction. This new Asperion was a stranger; it would tell him nothing, in any case.

Sylvan strode forward, moving past Thorne. And before he could second guess it, he put his hands on Flint's shoulders and pushed him out of the circle.

Flint struck out as if to grab hold of Sylvan, lunging for the knife he kept at his belt beside his own vial of magepool water. Sylvan tried to block him, but he moved with unnatural swiftness, freeing the blade before Sylvan could stop him. If Asperion wished to have Sylvan murdered, this would be the way. With the entire court here to see that it had been Flint.

Under thrall or not, he would be punished. But it wouldn't matter. Sylvan would be dead.

Sylvan raised his hands, ready to push his aura forward and end Flint's thrall.

But Asperion anticipated him. "Wait," he commanded.

Sylvan would not have heeded him, but he was ill prepared to match Flint's speed. Before he could snatch the knife away, Flint applied it to his own wrist and slashed.

The knife sank in deep, dragging the flesh apart. Sylvan

lurched forward, knocking the knife from Flint's hand, but blood was already spilling down his arm, soaking his sleeve.

And Sylvan didn't know how he heard it. But down the row of humans, a woman gasped.

It was such a strange, horrified sound in comparison to the impressed murmurs of the crowd—those who dared make any noise at all—and Sylvan could not stop himself from looking to see who had made it.

It was *her*. The woman from last night, the one who'd released the shimmerlings. He looked at her just in time to see the open horror on her face, before she wiped it away. But her bottom lip was trembling, her fists clenched at her sides.

The thrall wasn't holding her. Why wasn't the thrall holding her?

Flint collapsed to his knees, dragging Sylvan's attention away from the woman.

"Amazing, King Asperion. You've broken my best valet." His voice was a dry rasp of a sound, revealing far more of his discomfort than he would have liked. He couldn't quite puzzle together how the king intended to use this in practice, but perhaps that didn't matter.

Sylvan looked to the nearest poison-speaker, a black-haired mage with a thick beard. "A healer. Now."

The poison-speaker glanced at the king, then back at Sylvan. When Asperion did not object, he stepped away from his post. No doubt they both assumed the healer would be too late.

Sylvan assumed the same. What good were his powers, any of them, when healing wasn't among them?

When he turned his back on Flint to meet the king's gaze, Asperion was looking at him with narrow-eyed suspicion. Thorne still stood several paces behind him, his shoulders rounded slightly, his face gone gray.

"Prince Thorne," Asperion said, still holding Sylvan's gaze.

"Your brother was eager to demonstrate the power of the enthrallment. You will now take your turn."

There was a glint in his eye that Sylvan dislike. One he feared.

King Asperion pointed down the line of humans. "Her next."

Sylvan didn't have to look to know that he was pointing at the woman who'd released the shimmerlings, the one who'd spoken to him so fearlessly last night. The one who very clearly, at least to Sylvan, was not currently held in thrall. Did the king suspect as much? Or had Sylvan's gaze merely lingered on her for too long?

Thorne swallowed hard and took a step forward.

This time, Sylvan knew exactly what he was doing as he blocked his brother for the second time. "Not this one," he said. "This one is mine."

CHAPTER SEVEN

NEVE

"This one is mine."

Blood and sweat mingled in the air, twisting Neve's stomach into knots that made her fear she'd be sick. Not that there was much in her stomach after a night spent in the dungeons. But if she lost control, she would betray herself. They would all know that the thrall couldn't hold her, couldn't control her body.

She couldn't help but think that, for once, it might be a mercy to be held in thrall. For perhaps the first time in her life, she envied the humans who stood beside her, still as statues and unaware that one of their own lay dying on the cobblestones.

The man might have slashed the knife into his own veins, but Neve knew who to blame.

Sylvan Everstone stood before her once again, his hair blazing in the sunlight, the rich red color a striking contrast to the pallor of his skin. Where the other mages were dressed in an array of garish colors, his jacket was of the deepest black. It hugged his broad shoulders, the close cut following the slim taper of his waist. Neve had never thought of him as a large man, but now he seemed to loom over her like a giant.

This one is mine. His words hung in the courtyard, and she could practically feel the crowd of mages leaning forward to see what would happen next.

He would never let her go. Not easily. He was still angry about the shimmerlings, surely, and about her refusal to take a job as his 'servant.' He wished to punish her... but did he truly wish her dead? As far as he knew, one shove out of the circle would result in her tearing her own veins to shreds.

And she had no idea what she would do, if it came to that.

King Asperion barked a laugh. It was a harsh, tearing sort of a sound. Far different from his reputation for boisterous, drunken guffaws. "Yours, you say? You, who are too good to bed hollows, have taken one as your whore?"

Neve expected Sylvan to correct him. To say that no, he simply meant that he wanted to be the instrument of her destruction.

And she couldn't keep her cheeks from reddening when he did no such thing. When he just stood there, looking at her, failing to deny it.

He... he *was* claiming her as his whore? Certainly humans fulfilled such roles, both under thrall and without it, or so it was claimed. But Prince Sylvan *was* known for his disdain of humans. Even had he not been, it was clear enough; his own servant lay dying before him, and he didn't so much as glance in the man's direction. He was cold. Heartless. He was the monster they whispered about in the streets.

His protection, he'd offered her. As if she were a fool.

In the crowd, a throat cleared. "Prince Sylvan did... he did claim her yesterday. As well."

Neve allowed her gaze to flicker toward the voice. Evander, the human-torturing mage. Excellent. Probably trying to garner favor after attracting Sylvan's ire yesterday.

Though judging by the way the Soulslayer's eyes narrowed, he didn't trust the man any more than she did.

Neve didn't know how to read the expression on his face. His slate-gray eyes might have been forged from stone, for all they revealed. He moved close to her, leaning down as if to bury his nose in her hair.

But to Neve's surprise, he left a gap between them. A whisper of space. "Play along." He spoke the words into her ear, his breath hot against her skin, and she shivered. Did she have a choice?

The healer had arrived, and he knelt in a puddle of blood beside the fallen servant. The smell of it rose up to choke her, thick and coppery. There were four more humans lined up for slaughter.

And Neve. The courtesan. The plaything.

The whore.

Still, she nodded. Just the barest twitch of a movement. She wasn't even sure that Sylvan had seen, until he twisted a lock of her hair gently around one finger, then turned to face the king. "I like her hair," he said.

King Asperion laughed again, but his mirth felt forced. "You're not as weak as I'd imagined." The king waved his hand, as if it were nothing to him. "Fine. Your toy may live. For now."

Neve couldn't help feeling like she'd been dropped directly into a pit of hissing vipers. For the moment, they were more concerned with one another than they were with her. But that couldn't last.

Prince Thorne cleared his throat. "A remarkable feat, Father. And they will remain enthralled when you leave for the Miragelands?"

Incredible, that she'd been allowed to witness this revelation. To learn that the mages didn't lock themselves in the fortress every three years at all. Rather, they left the Vales completely, all of them, to visit their native Miragelands. To recharge their magic.

She didn't know what she was supposed to do with that information, but for now, it was enough that she knew it.

Sylvan moved close to her once again, and Asperion's reply was drowned beneath the roar of her own thoughts. Would the Soulslayer truly attempt to take her to his bed? Or did he have other tortures planned for her?

He reached down and took her hand, his fingers entwining with hers. She would have expected them to be cold and bony, unyielding. But his skin was warm in spite of his paleness, his grip strong and sure.

As he pulled her out of the circle and tucked her against his side, she wondered if she was meant to try to hurt herself. Perhaps it was reckless and stupid, and perhaps she would regret it, but in this moment, she would rather give away her immunity than play their game so fully that she killed herself in the process.

If she did that, she might as well be under thrall. She might as well be as trapped as every other human in the Vales.

But those watching must have assumed she was under Sylvan's thrall now, rather than King Asperion's. It was strange how they looked away when he approached, how their attention stayed a touch *too* focused on the king. Neve didn't like Sylvan, but there was no denying his power when he entered a room. He drew her focus like a magnet, and it was strange to her that no one else seemed to look his way. Their gazes slid past him, as though he did not exist at all.

Though they gave themselves away by shuffling out of his path. They feared the Soulslayer, even if they didn't respect him.

As soon as they stepped into the empty halls of the fortress, Neve wrenched her hand out of Sylvan's grip, putting deliberate space between his body and hers. However gentle he might be acting with her, he was still a murderer. And she couldn't forget it. "You killed that man," she said.

"Don't be a fool." He paused, running a hand over his fore-head. "I... I didn't know that would happen."

Neve didn't believe him. His grief, his regret, was nothing more than a performance. She could run now, sprint down this hall and make it to the back garden and the gate he'd shown her. Had it only been yesterday? It felt like an age.

Sylvan didn't touch her again, but she could tell he had read her intentions from the way he positioned himself between her body and the long expanse of hallway. "If you run, they'll kill you before you reach the gates."

He spoke softly, but his voice was rough and deep, as though he used it but rarely. Surely that couldn't be true. Powerful men were always talking about their power. At length.

"Even the secret gate?" Neve spat back.

"It was unguarded, not secret. There's a difference."

Neve knew she'd be a fool to disbelieve him. Mysterious though his motives were, he'd saved her back in the courtyard. Just as he'd saved her last night. After a moment, she nodded.

She'd thought he would lead her to the tower she'd breached last night, the one with the now empty shimmerling cages. He and Prince Thorne had descended from there, so she'd assumed they both kept their chambers in the tower.

Instead, Sylvan turned down a corridor before they reached the landing from yesterday, leading her deeper into the interior veins of the fortress.

The inside of the castle was not, to her surprise, the dour and forbidding place she'd assumed it would be. She supposed she wasn't sure exactly what she expected—bones and darkness and tapestries depicting violent scenes—but there were more paintings than wall hangings, most of them landscapes. A cheerful number of torches dotted the walls, and the sun leaked in from a surprising number of windows, including those that led to courtyard-facing balconies.

The place did not smell of must and blood, but of fresh air.

Sunlight. And, in the background, that ever present cloying mess of sugar. But it was fainter here, replaced by warmth and... livability.

Sylvan led her to a door on the second floor and opened it without ceremony, ushering her into a spacious sitting room.

The door on the opposite wall opened into the bedroom.

As soon as the door was shut, he turned to her, studying her like a puzzle he'd been working too long to solve. Still, he did not touch her. Had not touched her since she'd wrenched her hand out of his, yet she could still feel the phantom pressure of his grip.

"Are you immune?" he asked.

The room tilted, and she blinked, trying to will away the fear. It was one thing to suspect that he had guessed; it was another to have him say it out loud.

Neve *never* admitted it out loud. Not in adulthood, anyway. Not to anyone. Humans who knew could not be trusted. And the mages, well. Mercy was hardly in their nature.

Her silence seemed to irritate him, and he stalked closer, lips pulled into a solemn line, a lock of red hair falling across his forehead. She had the absurd urge to brush it aside, and she clenched her fists, pressing her nails into her palms to stop herself from doing anything so stupid. This was Sylvan Everstone. This was the *Soulslayer*.

"Are. You. Immune?" he repeated. "To the thrall?"

She pushed her chin up and met his gray gaze. If she could not find her courage, then she would at least pretend that she had. "Enthrall me and find out."

He stared at her. She could get lost in those eyes, if she made herself meet them for long enough. Lost like an explorer setting off to distant lands, her ship lost on stormy seas for all eternity. She shivered, gripping her upper arms tight as if it could ward off a chill that no breeze had wrought.

Perhaps he *was* trying to enthrall her. His aura hadn't

changed, but his powers were the subject of legends, of awed whispers in the streets. He might be able to control the appearance of his aura. He might be able to enthrall her when no one else could.

And yet she stood free. No haze, no listlessness, no sudden urge to touch her toes. Or hold a blade to her own wrists. "Was that man really your servant?" she heard herself ask.

He stood frighteningly still. Like a predator watching its prey from the reeds. "How did you accomplish it?" he asked, ignoring her question.

Neve wanted to press him for an answer, to demand he explain how he could have promised her his protection only last night, when this morning his own servant lay dead in the courtyard. She had little faith that even a mage healer could have worked fast enough to save the poor man.

But the intensity of his gaze stilled her tongue. What was it about this man that made her forget her own survival? Her entire life had been a study in shutting her mouth, in pretending to be meek while seething inside, in taking what petty revenge she could muster—but in the shadows, only. In safety, only.

This man had thrown her out into the blazing sun.

He was still waiting for her answer. No lie would stand up to the intensity of that stare, let alone the questions that would follow. He already knew, had already seen. It would do no good to lie.

"I have been immune since birth," she said.

"Impossible." He spit the word out like a curse.

She should have been afraid. Instead, she was annoyed. She propped her fists on her hips. "Yet here I stand before you, Soulslayer."

"Most people would not dare speak to me that way."

"Most people are fools."

The corner of his mouth twitched, as if he might actually express an emotion. As if it might be amusement, of all things.

Not that Neve thought him capable of that. "What is your name?" he asked.

That, at least, she could answer without restraint. "Neve Iriam."

"And who else knows of these unique abilities of yours, Neve Iriam?"

She hesitated. This time, the truth would cost more than she was willing to give. "No one."

But Sylvan was watching her too closely. And reading her too well. He narrowed his eyes. "Try again."

She let out a breath. "My mother knew. But she is... not an issue. Anymore."

Not a lie. It sounded like something it wasn't, but it wasn't a lie.

Sylvan bowed his head. "I am sorry for your loss."

He assumed she meant her mother was dead, and that had been the point. The surprise, the infinite surprise, was that he was *sorry* about it. Enough that he would bother to share his condolences with a mere human.

Enough to take a step toward her, eyes locked on hers. He lifted his hand, slowly, as if he meant to touch her cheek. Or perhaps brush aside a rogue lock of hair.

And she found she could not draw away. Not because of any enthrallment, but because of some curiosity she dared not name.

"My brother and I are attempting to banish the mages from your lands," he said. His voice was little more than a whisper, barely audible.

Her lips parted, surprise snatching any response she might have tried to make. *Her* lands? As in the humans' lands?

"You may be able to help us," he continued. "If we can figure out the source of your immunity, and whether it can be shared with others."

She wanted to laugh. She wanted to cry. Her immunity had

been tested, at length and against her will, for years. Years upon years. "Why would you think I can help with that?"

"Because," he said, his voice rough, "I am out of other options."

And she was the one he had left? She wanted to laugh. She wanted to cry. "I need time to consider."

Sylvan took a step closer, so close now that she could feel the heat of his body. So close that if she moved, at all, their bodies would be flush against one another. "I would give you that time, if I could. But King Asperion… he'll be angry about today. He'll be on his way here, even now, to ensure that…" He cleared his throat, and Neve swore there were spots of color heating his cheeks. "We must make some… display. If our ruse is to be believed."

Spots of heat bloomed on her own cheeks as she understood his meaning. If the king suspected that Sylvan had lied about their relationship, about his claim on her—his desire for her— then Neve's life would be forfeit. And his hope of purging his kind from the Vales would be dead.

Why he would want to do such a thing—why could be explained later. *Why* did not matter right in this moment, with footsteps now audible in the corridor outside the chamber. *Why* was a question for later.

Sylvan must have taken her silence for hesitation, because he added, "There will be no need for you to take it any further than you wish. Than either of us should wish." His flush deepened. "But I would not… I will not kiss you without your leave."

Heat pooled in Neve's belly, desire tracing a hot line through her core. What in the demons was wrong with her? This was to be a ruse. A performance. Yet she could not wrench her gaze away from his lips.

"For a world without mages," she breathed, "I can pretend to be your whore."

Sylvan lifted a hand to her cheek, brushing her hair away

69

from her face. He leaned toward her, and she could almost believe the king was already watching by the way he breathed in, long and deep.

It felt real. Like he was inhaling her very essence. And right now, in this moment, it *was* real. His gaze was on her lips, his breath mingled with hers, and her senses were full of the smell of spicy cedarwood.

His hand fell to her hip, and his lips met hers in a touch that was anything but soft. Every protest in her mind that said this was all for show fell away as he groaned into her mouth, the resonance of his want stoking the fire of her own. He pressed closer, pushing her against the wall, and she could feel the hard length of his desire against her body, proving that in one way, at least, this moment was very real indeed.

He wanted her.

Her thoughts were smoke, all reason fled from her mind and certainly from her body as she responded to the prince's touch. In a moment, the door would open. When it did, this would cease.

She wished that it never would. She was made of want, despite everything she knew of this man.

Sylvan's hand rose to her breast, skimming along the hard peak of her nipple, and her legs nearly gave way beneath her. Had he not been pinning her to the wall, his knee wedged between her legs, she would have fallen. She arched into him, dragging her body along his, aching for some release. He pressed closer, urging her on as he deepened the kiss, tasting her, claiming her mouth the way his words had claimed her in the courtyard.

The door slammed open, and Neve startled, but Sylvan did not stop. She might as well have been truly in his thrall, for all that she would have let him take her right there, audience or no.

King Asperion cleared his throat, and Sylvan finally broke

the kiss, though he did not break the close proximity of their bodies, nor did he drop his hand from her breast. He might have ripped her clothing away, might have made it more believable still, yet he left her entirely covered. Covered and quivering and wishing she were bare before him.

She shook her head, willing her senses to return. This was not some one-night release, some stranger met over drinks in a tavern.

For a start, no one-night release had ever kissed her like that.

"I want you at tomorrow's council meeting," Asperion said.

Sylvan let his hand fall from her breast, skimming along the side of her body as he pressed another kiss to her lips. "A personal summons," he murmured. "Must be important."

"It is, boy."

Sylvan stepped away from her, and she nearly stumbled at the loss of his support. She made a show of pushing her skirts down over her legs and readjusting her bodice. Not that it mattered; the king's attention was locked on the prince.

Behind him, though, two guards hovered in the doorway. One of them gave her a leering sort of grin when she caught his eye, but she looked away quickly. A human in thrall would not throw out a rude gesture. Much though she might wish to.

"What is the topic of this all-important meeting, I wonder?" Sylvan strode casually toward a cabinet against the far wall, as if he'd been interrupted while reading a book rather than ravishing the woman he'd claimed as his whore. He opened the cabinet and pulled out a decanter of wine. His hand was far steadier than Neve's would have been.

Probably he pulled ruses like this all the time. Probably his days were full of women. He would be having no trouble recovering from the rapid thrum of his heartbeat, nor the unsatisfied ache of desire.

Instead of answering the question, Asperion motioned to his

guards. They preceded him out the door as if expecting an assassin to appear from around the first bend in the stairs. Though the leering one did throw a final wink over his shoulder before the door slammed shut behind them.

Leaving Neve alone in the chamber with Prince Sylvan. Silence stretched between them, and though they were now separated by the expanse of the room, she could still feel the press of his body against hers, the grip of his fingers on her hip.

Sylvan held a glass of wine out to her. "Are you all right?"

As if she had played no part in what had just happened between them. Surely he could not think her so good an actress.

Because it *was* a ruse, a voice in the back of her mind insisted. Her senses, perhaps, returning at last. It was a ruse, and Sylvan was a convincing liar. He would have to be, if he'd been scheming to banish his people to another world. Their home world, if he could be believed, though legend said it had been rendered unlivable.

So, no. She was not all right, though not for the reasons he assumed.

And for reasons she had no interest in exploring, it made her furious.

She strode over to him and snatched the glass from his hands. "You may sleep on the settee tonight."

With more effort than she wanted to admit, she backed away from him, clutching the wine like a lifeline, and shut herself inside his bedchamber.

CHAPTER EIGHT

NEVE

*N*eve had to admit that she hated Prince Sylvan slightly less when she woke the next morning to find a steaming bath waiting for her in the sitting room. Petals of aromatic flowers floated on the surface, letting off gentle scents of rose oil and lilies. She'd slept in her dungeon-filthy clothes, and she stripped eagerly, without concern for what she would wear when she emerged. She stepped into the water, allowing her legs to grow accustomed to the heat before lowering the rest of her body in after them. Her skin tingled with pleasure, muscles releasing their long-held tension in response to the pleasant heat. She let her arms float, reveling in the weightless feeling of it.

She didn't know how long the bath had been sitting here, or what magic the mages must have used on it to keep the water burning hot, but she intended to stay submerged for the rest of the day, breathing in the sweetness of it.

A sharp knock came on the door, and she sank deeper into the water, expecting Sylvan—they were his rooms, whether he'd ordered a bath or not—or perhaps even King Asperion's leering guard.

"Come back later," she said, though anyone in the fortress who wanted to enter could no doubt do so, whether she gave her permission or not.

"I assume that means you're bathing," a woman replied. "I brought you some clean clothes. May I enter? I promise to divert my gaze."

Neve had less concern for her modesty than for her life. The woman might be an assassin, or a kidnapper.

Though most likely, she was merely a human servant.

"Who are you?" she asked.

"Will you believe me if I say I'm a friend?"

"Will you go away if I say no?"

The door opened, and the woman stepped into the room, smiling cheerfully. It was at once apparent that she was no human servant, but a mage—one of the nobility, at that. She wore a garishly purple dress, her black hair tied into an efficient coil of braids at the back of her head.

Against Neve's very best intentions, she liked the woman immediately.

"Afraid I can't," the woman said. "I'm to parade you about the castle and teach you how to behave. So you don't run into any trouble."

Too late for that. "Any *more* trouble," Neve grumbled.

The woman winked. "Indeed. Come on, out with you."

"I haven't even washed yet."

The woman set her hands on her hips, calling to mind the schoolteachers Neve had met when she was a child. It had been a long time since she'd had any proper schooling, but she remembered that posture well enough. "What *have* you been doing?"

Neve dropped her head back until only her face was visible above the water. If she lived in the fortress, she would call for a bath every single day. Twice a day. "Wallowing."

The woman waved her hand dismissively. "That is unacceptable. Soap up, now. We've no time for self pity."

"Are you a governess?" Neve grumbled.

"No. I am something worse. I'm Lady Dahlia Ammond. Now wash, before I have you flayed for disobeying."

She said it cheerfully, but something about the businesslike clip of her tone said she would haul Neve out of the water with her own hands, if she took much longer. She grabbed the soap and started to scrub her legs.

When she was satisfied with Neve's cleanliness, Lady Dahlia helped her out of the bath, holding out a towel. Neve wrapped herself in it gratefully, enjoying the soft caress of the fabric against her skin.

She would not have expected any mage to serve the needs of a human this way—that was why they had human servants in the first place—but certainly there must be someone other than this courtier.

Unless Sylvan wanted to torture this woman. If so, it wasn't working; she was clearly unfazed by the assignment.

Dahlia bustled to the pile of dresses she'd brought with her, selecting a green one from the top and holding it up in front of Neve's body. She nodded her approval and, to Neve's surprise, stepped aside for her to see as well. As if Neve, too, should have a say in which of these impossibly beautiful gowns she would wear today.

The green dress she'd chosen was practically glowing, the ribbons tracing up the bodice in an intricate crisscrossing pattern that covered much more skin than Neve would have anticipated. Unless she was mistaken, the dress had more than enough fabric to cover her bosom. There were no untoward slits, the skirts designed to puff rather than cling to her shape.

"Is it…" She cleared her throat. "Is it the kind of thing a courtesan would wear?"

Dahlia clucked her tongue. "I'm sure *I* don't know. But you're not going out there to bed the entire court. You're going out to be seen by them. Besides, as far as they know, you belong to him. They won't bat an eye at his jealousy. He keeps to himself."

Neve was pretty sure they'd expect to *see* a lot more of her than this dress allowed. She wasn't going to complain, though.

"As for your question, I'm here because Sylvan trusts me," Dahlia said. "I'm only half mage, you see. But *that* is a secret, so do keep it between us, if you don't mind."

She spoke matter-of-factly, so much so that it made Neve wonder if she could be covering some other emotion. She'd never thought about half mages before, never even considered that they might exist. Was that the reason for her apparent shield of forthrightness? Any such children would certainly be hesitant to advertise their origins.

Or... could this woman be his lover? Heat crawled up Neve's neck, a confusing mixture of guilt and some other, more twisted emotion that she didn't care to name.

She stepped into the dress, pulling it up over her shoulders. "Do you always tell your secrets to perfect strangers?"

Dahlia stepped over and began to help with the laces, her fingers fast and dextrous. "Only the ones Sylvan claims as his."

His. Not his courtesan, not his whore, just... his. "And does that happen often?"

"Never."

Curious, that Dahlia lived her life as a titled mage, her human blood kept secret. Had some high-up mage actually claimed her as their daughter, hiding the human part of her heritage?

"Does the thrall work on you?" Neve asked.

An impertinent question. But then, Dahlia was the kind of person who invited instant familiarity.

"I'm susceptible to it," Dahlia replied airily. "That's why I visit him."

Neve shook her head, confused, and Dahlia frowned at her in the mirror. "Sylvan doesn't enthrall humans," she explained. "Not ever. I come to him so that he may break any thrall someone else might have put on me. It happens only incidentally, when I pass too close to a relic. Sylvan erases it."

And she trusted him to do so. To keep her secret while ensuring her freedom. It was a fact that did not match with the man Neve had seen.

Or did it? Prince Sylvan hadn't punished Neve for releasing the shimmerlings; he'd intervened with Evander and helped her escape. He'd prevented her injury yesterday, when the king had been prepared to execute her.

But Sylvan had been clear about his reasoning for that. He'd figured out her secret, and he wanted to use her immunity to help him banish the mages from the Vales. Why, she did not yet know. But she couldn't pretend it wasn't an intriguing prospect.

Perhaps most notably of all? He'd asked her permission. He could have forced her, thrall or no. Instead, he'd invited her to be his ally.

The surprise must have been evident on her face, though the long silence was perhaps more telling.

"You didn't realize?" Dahlia tilted her head. "I wonder at it. I would have expected him to tell you... but then, most humans wouldn't believe it, I suppose. Especially one he'd claimed as his..." She trailed off.

"Toy," Neve finished for her.

Dahlia lifted a shoulder, still brushing Neve's hair. "That is one term." For a few minutes, she focused on the twist of Neve's hair, her fingers soft and dextrous.

When she was done, she patted Neve's shoulder. "Come," she said. "We have promenading to do."

—*—

Neve's first introduction to the gardens had been quick and furtive, punctuated by the glow of escaping shimmerlings and the press of Sylvan's fingertips on her arm.

Now, in the afternoon sunlight, the grounds might have been another world entirely. Enormous blossoms filled every tree, bush, and stem, so heavy that they bent their supporting branches toward the meandering brick paths. In the darkness, the place had felt close and heady; in the light, it was expansive and alive. She felt as if she'd stepped inside a world made of stained glass.

Mages strolled along the paths in groups of twos and threes, eyeing one another while pretending to enjoy the gardens. Though as soon as any of them caught sight of Neve walking among them, they forgot their mage rivals and focused their attention on her. She'd never quite understood the idea that a person could physically feel another's gaze locked on them. Now, though, she had to admit that their stares were very weighty indeed.

Dahlia strolled along by her side, smiling and waving to each of them. Neve's tongue burned with unasked questions, but it was still difficult to know which ones she could risk without offending the one person who seemed eager to help her. Though no doubt she was doing so for her own reasons.

Neve decided that, if she could not ask a prying question about Dahlia's life, then she'd ask one about Sylvan's.

"Prince Sylvan," she said as they passed a group of four mages who'd stopped to nod to them. "Where did he go? For those three years?"

"That," Dahlia replied, "is hardly my story to tell."

So much for that idea. It was worth a try, though. Sylvan was hardly likely to be forthcoming about his own story, even if she did find the courage to ask him. She didn't know if it was one of those secrets that was common knowledge among the mages—like this apparent every-three-year return to the Miragelands—or whether it was a secret from them as well.

A group of women rounded the turn in front of them, led by the one Neve recognized as Evander's partner in coal-feeding torture yesterday. Her chestnut tresses were coiled around her head in an intricate design of loops and braids that still left half of her thick curls free to rest upon one shoulder. She wore a crimson gown, the shoulders so low that Neve wondered her pale skin did not immediately redden in the sun.

Dahlia bent her head closer to Neve's. "First lesson: smile."

"I smile."

"You glower." She gave Neve's arm a pinch. "Whatever Fern and her minions say to you, they are not saying it to *you*. They are saying it to Sylvan Soulslayer's mistress."

Neve rubbed her arm. "It's the same thing."

"No. *You* are a person. *She* is a symbol. The secret to a thick skin is knowing the skin they aim to pierce isn't even yours."

It was easy for her to say, Neve thought as Fern and her friends stopped before them. Fern gave Neve an appraising look, as if she were still deciding what strategy to take. Her friends seemed likely to follow whatever lead she showed them. They clustered around her, mimicking the jut of her hip so closely that it might have been choreographed.

But Fern's attention slipped away from Neve quickly, as if she were not worth the time. It settled, instead, on Dahlia. "Lady Dahlia," she said, her voice warm and smooth. "Still considering yourself part of the court, I see, even with Lord Ammond two years gone."

The women who were with her twittered like birds, though the closest one covered her mouth as if she could not quite believe Fern had said such a thing in Dahlia's presence. But the glitter in her eyes said she was enjoying every morsel.

There were so many undercurrents at work here. Neve felt like she'd been thrown out to sea without a rescue line.

Dahlia gave the women a sweet smile, as though Fern had complimented her dress or commented on the weather. "I am akin to a persistent fungus, in that way."

A surprised laugh bubbled through Neve's lips before she could stop it, and Dahlia's smile widened. Fern crossed her arms, making a point not to look at Neve. "I doubt Lord Ammond would rejoice in your choice of companion."

"Oh, decidedly not." Dahlia might have been praising Fern's taste in footwear, or her latest card-game win. Or whatever else it was that mages did in their free time. "Lord Ammond would have me locked in the dungeon for even speaking to a human. Thank goodness he's nothing more than ash in the wind."

Fern blinked, slowly, as if trying to decide whether Dahlia had made a joke. She certainly made it sound as if she had, but Never had the feeling she meant every word.

Dahlia patted her arm. "This is Neve, by the way."

Fern glanced at Neve, then turned her attention to a nearby blossom, running her fingers along its buttery petals. "Yes. Prince Sylvan's taste in women is exactly as abysmal as I would have expected."

The woman beside her, the one who'd covered her mouth, actually glanced over her shoulder. The other women's expressions were similarly shocked. If Prince Sylvan were to appear from around the corner, they would no doubt simper and protest about the lighthearted jokes they made while promenading.

Neve had always thought Sylvan Everstone to be as feared among the mages as he was among humans. But Evander had been willing to insult him openly—even if Sylvan's arrival in the hall had clearly frightened him—and now Fern was doing the same.

Neve opened her mouth to respond, but Dahlia squeezed her arm tighter. A reminder. That to Fern, Neve was a symbol. Nothing more.

Judging by the way Fern was looking at Neve now, it made no difference to her. If she could, she'd take Neve down just for the pleasure of it.

A symbol she might be, but a symbol made of flesh could still bleed.

But Neve clamped her teeth together, if only for the simple fact that she was supposed to be under at least some level of thrall. A pliant human, ready to be molded to their will.

Fern started forward, making a point to brush past Neve despite the ample width of the path. "Good luck, dear. At least your torment will not last long. Sylvan will soon tire of you, and you'll be out in the cold. Or, you'll be dead."

She sauntered away, her entourage strutting after her and exchanging glances that said they'd be discussing this conversation for the rest of the afternoon.

As Neve watched them go, a shadowy figure caught her eye as it hurried along the far walkway, the one that ran along the back wall. While the mages made a point of luxuriously slow strolls, this person walked with quick, furtive steps. He had no mage's aura. Which meant he must be human.

When he caught sight of Neve, he stopped and held her gaze. And then he nodded.

Neve looked at Dahlia. "Would it be all right if I took one turn alone?"

"After that interaction? Truly?" Dahlia brushed her hands on her skirts, then sidled over to a bench. "You're braver than I. All right. I shall wait for you here."

Neve nodded her thanks before striding along the path toward the garden wall, pausing occasionally to inspect a flower or peer into a fountain. Finally she slipped out of sight behind a hedge. There was a small fountain here, three tiers rising out of a stone basin like cake made of obsidian. The trickle of the water nearly drowned the distant notes of laughter and conversation, though the notes of birdsong were decidedly louder here. As if the creatures had decided they were safer away from the mages.

The stranger was there, leaning over to skim his fingertips across the surface of the fountain's pool. His hair was long, light brown and streaked with blond, as though he'd spent many hours in the sun, and his nose was thin and bold. She realized with a start that he must be the person who'd been waiting for her outside her rooms on the night she'd released the shimmerlings.

Not one of Sylvan's minions, but a human. Who was he?

"The blossoms in this garden unnerve me," he said. "They're practically large enough to sit in."

She let out a breath. "You're not under thrall."

She couldn't quite say how she knew. Years of study, perhaps. Of watching people like Lydia snap out of the thrall, or watching it leak away as their relics lost potency.

His eyes met hers. "Nor are you."

For a moment, she held his gaze, the truth stretching between them. Neither of them had confirmed it; neither of them needed to.

"You have an unprecedented opportunity, Neve Iriam," he said.

He knew her name. He knew where she lived. And he had no trouble getting into the fortress gardens. Who was this man? "What do you mean?" she asked.

He dipped his fingers back into the flow of the fountain. "There are those among the humans who would break free of the mages. Who would rid us of these oppressors. And now you find yourself in their innermost circle."

She'd heard similar words spoken all her life, by people who claimed that their interests aligned with hers. By people who claimed that all human interests ought to align with hers.

But everyone who'd ever known the truth about her had ultimately attempted to bleed her dry.

This man knew that Sylvan had claimed her as his whore, but he had no idea it was only a ruse. He thought Sylvan was taking her against her will. That she was a prisoner. And his first thought was how he could use her.

This was why Neve had learned to be selfish. Because if she didn't protect herself, care for herself, then no one else would.

"Who are you?" she asked.

His lips curved upwards, but she could hardly call it a smile. "Nobody. At least, not anymore."

She waited.

"My ancestors were kings," he said after a moment. "The Vales had them, once. Human kings and queens. If you can believe it."

What a thought. As if ancient history had any bearing on the present. She didn't care who his ancestors were, centuries upon centuries ago. "I only care who you are now."

"You can call me Darius."

It told her very little. But it was a start. "Are we the only ones?" she asked. "With immunity?"

She'd searched. Demons, how she'd searched.

"There's another. Shall I tell her you'll help us?"

"No," Neve said. "Since you haven't even told me what it is you wish to do."

Darius made a sound of disgust. "Surely you aren't looking to *protect* him? He believes he's taking you into his bed under thrall, that you are neither willing nor—"

"I know what he believes," she interrupted. "I need to get back, before I'm missed."

With that, she turned her back on him, heading back out toward the main part of the garden.

"Think on it," Darius called after her. "But don't wait too long. I would not want you to get caught in the oncoming storm."

CHAPTER NINE

SYLVAN

*S*ylvan hadn't spoken with Thorne since the demonstration. He'd hoped to pull his brother aside after King Asperion's council meeting, but the session had droned on and on as advisor after advisor bowed and scraped and praised the king for his heroic plan to save them all from the necessity of returning to the Miragelands. Thorne had somehow managed to slip away before the last one finished, with Asperion apparently none the wiser.

Though given the king's alarming talent for acting and subterfuge, Sylvan wouldn't have counted on it.

Sylvan had bullied his way into Thorne's rooms this morning after a second restless night spent on the settee, all too aware of Neve's presence on the other side of his bedroom door, imagining the taste of citrus and herbs and salt, of late summer nights spent under the stars.

That kiss had been nothing like he'd expected. Nothing. The kiss that was supposed to have been a ruse, yet had kept him awake and tossing through the nights that'd followed, taking himself into his own hand and hoping to forget her even as he imagined that his grip belonged to her, that her moans of pleasure were joining his in the dark.

He could not deny that he'd wanted to kiss her since their very first meeting, but the fire she'd brought to it, the way her body had responded to his... It made him hard just to think about the way her body had writhed beneath his. The way she'd parted her lips to slide her tongue hungrily against his. The supple softness of her breast in his hand, her gasp as he'd stroked the hard peak of her nipples. The way she'd looked at him with those vivid green eyes, like she wanted more of him.

But that was a fallacy. A lie he was telling himself. No one wanted him, and desire was a weakness he could not risk.

And so he'd done the logical thing. He'd avoided her. Hadn't seen her, in fact, since she'd flounced into his bedchamber, claiming it as her own.

It wasn't the most strategic move, when the entire court was meant to believe he was bedding her. The problem was, he couldn't stop thinking about *actually* bedding her. Though, he wasn't feeling overly particular about the location. He'd imagined continuing that kiss, uninterrupted, until she parted her thighs for him to take her against the wall. He'd imagined bending her over the desk, laying her down on the settee. Watching from the floor as she rode him from above.

He'd worked tirelessly to master his emotions, his desires. His actions, certainly.

One kiss, and this woman was tearing it all down.

Hence his need to find his brother. The sooner they could fix their plans, the sooner he could send her on her way. And if it seemed unlikely that he could ever forget she existed, well, at least she'd have the chance to forget about *him*.

Thorne was seated by the fire with one leg thrown over the arm of his chair, the other stretched out before him. He held a goblet of wine in his hands, though it was still mid morning, his white knuckles belying his lazy smile. Sometimes it was difficult to remember that he was Sylvan's older brother, and not the other way around.

They'd been sitting here in silence since Sylvan's arrival, and it was becoming more and more evident that, for once, Thorne didn't intend to be the first to speak.

"Where have you been?" Sylvan asked. "You disappeared."

He had the distinct impression that his brother had been avoiding him.

"Simply mourning the death of our well-laid plans, brother," Thorne replied. "Surely you've been doing the same. I don't know about you, but I shall need a veritable army of concubines to erase the memory of all that blood. Two nights, and still it haunts me."

Thorne could put on all the performances he liked, but despite the callous boredom he tried to lace into his words, he was obviously agitated. He kept tapping his one foot on the floor, and if he kept squeezing the goblet with such force, he would eventually wear fingerprints into the thing.

Sylvan crossed his arms, waiting for the real answer.

Thorne dragged a hand through his hair, then dropped his head to rest on the back of the chair. "I did not need you to intervene. At the demonstration."

So Thorne *had* been avoiding him. It was a relief, actually, to know that not all of his instincts had betrayed him. Still, Sylvan had to work to restrain a scowl. "So you are comfortable being a murderer now?"

"We didn't know poor Flint would harm himself when Father gave that order," Thorne replied.

"But we knew he meant violence."

Flint lived, if barely. Sylvan had had his valet removed to a healer in the lower city. With luck, King Asperion would forget about the man entirely—he was a human and a prop, nothing more—but Sylvan didn't want to risk it. He'd failed, abysmally, at reading Asperion's intentions.

He had, however, sent a message to Flint's family, through the most secret channels he could access. Along with a hefty amount of coin.

"You put everything at risk when you took my place," Thorne said. "You drew his notice."

Sylvan paced to the window, his blood running too hot for rest. "He caught us off guard."

Thorne took a long drink from his goblet. "A true asp."

Indeed. Sylvan considered himself to be a patient person. A man who bided his time while plans that were years in the making moved ever so slowly toward fruition.

But the king had been hiding his true nature for an unbelievably long time. For Sylvan's entire life, though he couldn't help sifting through his memories for clues, for indications that Asperion was not the fool he'd always pretended to be.

It certainly made him wonder about the circumstances of his own abandonment in the Miragelands. He'd been caught in a sandstorm and left behind. Left for dead. He'd always assumed it to have been an accident. It hadn't occurred to him that anything else was possible. Whatever else Asperion was, Sylvan had never believed him to be a calculating man. He'd always been easily distractible, prone to drunkenness and buffoonery. Not that he'd ever been a kind man, exactly—though his cruelty toward humans was hardly a unique trait—only that he'd made himself into someone who was very easily dismissed.

It had been nothing but a trick. A con. One that Sylvan had fallen for all too easily.

Asperion might well have left Sylvan behind in the Miragelands on purpose, not expecting him to survive three years in that un-survivable place. Not expecting him to return with powers that eclipsed any ever seen before.

Asperion might even have arranged the death of Sylvan's mother, three years prior to that.

So, no. Sylvan did not believe that Asperion would reveal his true nature now simply to martyr himself to the Miragelands for the sake of his people.

"And now," Thorne said, "even *you* have taken a human lover, and—"

"I haven't." The words left his mouth before he could stop them, though if anyone knew the truth of his abhorrence for enthrallment, it was Thorne. "You know I've taken no human lovers."

Thorne tilted his head to the side. "Are you sure? Perhaps I should explain. When a man announces that a woman is his, *twice*, and goes on to explain to an entire assembly that he likes her hair, he is making it quite clear that he intends to bury his cock deep in her—"

"Stop." Sylvan shut his eyes. "I beg you."

"You? Beg? Impossible." When Sylvan opened his eyes again, Thorne was swirling the wine, watching him with open curiosity. He allowed himself another long draw before returning to the conversation. "She *is* the same woman who released the shimmerlings, is she not?"

He knew that she was. Sylvan leaned back against the window, doing everything in his power to shake the images that Thorne had brought rushing into his brain. The flood of *want*. Her hair felt like silk on his fingertips, and the slight inhalation of her breath before he'd kissed her... demons, he'd nearly come undone right there. He hadn't needed to pretend at all.

Had he been another man entirely, he'd have hauled her to his bed. He'd have taken her right there.

"It's all right, brother." Thorne's voice was offensively gentle. "It is understandable. She's quite pretty. And you're not the stone-hearted bastard they all think you are."

But he was.

"Thorne," Sylvan said, "I think she may be immune to the thrall."

He wasn't quite sure why he'd said it like that. He knew that she was. At least, he trusted that she'd told him the truth, not least because the evidence pointed directly to it. But then again, given what had happened with Asperion, Sylvan supposed it would be a good idea to put more emphasis on plain facts, and less on following his gut.

He could see by the way Thorne snapped his mouth shut that he'd been preparing another soliloquy, and that Sylvan had shocked him into silence. Temporary silence. Always temporary, with Thorne. "My dearest Sylvan," he said finally. "You do know that you have the power to *check*."

"No." The word slipped out of his mouth before he could stop it. "No. She would have to agree."

"The evil Soulslayer and his conscience," Thorne muttered. "If only the bards knew."

If the bards knew, then Sylvan would shred every one of their lutes. Before he could say as much, a knock sounded on the door.

Thorne sat up, dropping both feet to the ground. "That's her, isn't it?" he said. "You brought her *here*."

The door opened, and Dahlia sauntered into the room—not one to wait for leave to enter any room—followed by Neve.

She wore a gown of russet brown, enhancing the warm color of her skin. Her green eyes shone as if they were made of enchantments, and once he met them, it was difficult—near impossible—to look away. Unless it was to let his gaze fall to her lips.

"Gentlemen," Dahlia said cheerfully, "we know you were talking about us. That silence, my goodness. Might as well be shouting our names."

"Not you, darling," Thorne said. "Only your charming friend."

Dahlia blew him a kiss. Sylvan was never quite sure where those two stood with one another; she might just as well have thrown a knife at his head.

Sylvan drew a deep breath, attempting to shake off the spell of Neve's arrival. "We must get started," he said. "We need to learn as much as we can about Neve's immunity."

"Neve, is it?" Thorne said. "My brother isn't the best at making introductions."

Neve raised her eyebrows at him. "Neither are you, since you didn't give me *your* name."

Dahlia threw her head back and laughed. "He's so very arrogant, he assumes you already know it. This is Prince Thorne, whose name is appropriate since he will often intentionally irritate you until you wish you could wrench him out of your side and throw him into the rubbish bin."

"Welcome to the club," Thorne said drily. "Now if you will please stop tainting our new friend's opinion of me, I believe Sylvan has a task for us."

Dahlia set herself in the chair across from Thorne's, her back straight, gaze suddenly forthright. Sylvan always marveled at how quickly the woman could change direction. "There are only seven days until the Return," she said. "What if we *can't* learn enough in that time?"

"The answer is obvious," Thorne said finally, draining the last of his wine and setting the cup down with a loud clack. "In the case that we can't crack Neve's extraordinary abilities, we will have to settle for murdering the king."

CHAPTER TEN

NEVE

*B*y the time the sky outside Prince Thorne's windows darkened with oncoming night, Neve's head was throbbing from hours of discussion and planning and trying, however fruitlessly, to understand her powers. But a lifetime hadn't answered any of the questions these mages had for her, and wise as her new allies might be in the ways of magic, it was all too clear that they found themselves equally in the dark.

When the first stars began piercing their way into view, Thorne pressed his hands to the arms of his chair and heaved himself out of it, at once graceful and, she thought, slightly drunk. "I'm thoroughly beat," he said. "I must go to bed."

Sylvan paused his pacing to look at his brother, eyebrows raised. "These are *your* chambers. We can continue elsewhere."

But Thorne waved the suggestion away. "It's no matter, brother."

Neve wanted to ask where he expected to lay his head for the night. Before she could speak, Dahlia stood, too, stretching her arms over her head. "Which woman will it be tonight, then?"

Right. So he had plenty of options.

"I think," Thorne said, as though contemplating, "that I do not yet know her name."

The prince sounded casual, but he pointedly avoided looking at Dahlia as she arched deeper into her stretch, his jaw set so tightly he must be gritting his teeth. Given that Dahlia stood just a few paces from him, he practically had to crane his neck to keep from looking at her.

If Dahlia noted this, she didn't let on. "Truly?" she said. "I thought you'd bedded every willing skirt in the city by now."

Dahlia injected so much disbelief into her tone that it tipped over into something almost... caustic. Neve glanced at her, surprised. But Dahlia's face belied the sharpness of her tone, as if she were merely asking a friend about his plans for the evening with no concern for what his answer might be. When that plainly wasn't the case at all.

"There are still a *few* left, darling," Thorne replied.

Sylvan, who'd been hovering by the door, picked up a book from Thorne's shelf and began leafing through the pages. As though he'd heard this same conversation play out multiple times, and could not care less about the outcome.

Or perhaps it was awkwardness. If the Soulslayer were capable of feeling such a thing.

"Maybe," Dahlia went on, as though Thorne hadn't spoken, "you've merely forgotten their names. It would be understandable. I'm sure they wish they could forget yours, come to think of it."

Thorne opened the door. "Leave off, Dahlia. I'm quite overcome with fatigue."

She sauntered past him, hips swaying. "Poor baby. Not too fatigued to chase skirts, I hope."

"This is where you misunderstand the matter. I don't have to chase anyone. I'm so sweet that they come to me."

The door closed behind them, and Neve could still hear them trading jibes as their voices faded down the stairs. They'd worked perfectly well together all day, without so much as a hint of conflict. Yet the moment the work ended, they'd turned on one another like they were lifetime enemies. Dahlia hadn't even spoken to Fern like that when they'd met in the gardens, and the woman had spewed nothing but insults.

Sylvan leaned back against the window frame, the book still open in his hands. Neve doubted he had even the slightest idea of its contents.

"What was that about?" she asked.

He winced. "I find it's safest not to ask."

Clearly. "They must have some history."

"Or none at all."

"You never asked your brother?" She wasn't sure why she wanted to press the issue. Curiosity, in part, not only about Thorne and Dahlia but about Sylvan's relationship to the two of them.

He blinked at her, bemused. "Why would I do that?"

Men. Honestly. "Aren't you curious?"

Sylvan closed the book and set it back on the shelf. "You spent the day with my brother. If you think he holds back from discussing his trysts, despite my frequent objections, then you're far less observant than I would have expected. I have better things to do than get my head cut off for asking questions."

"The great Soulslayer, cowering in fear of his friends." The words left her mouth before she'd fully considered them, and she lifted her gaze to his, afraid of what his response might be. She must be exhausted, too, to have forgotten who he was. What he was capable of.

Though she had to admit that, so far, he hadn't shown any inclination to live up to his reputation. He was grumpy, perhaps. Intense, definitely. But cruel? She hadn't yet witnessed it.

Still. It would be best not to antagonize him.

To her surprise, his eyes glinted with amusement. There was even the barest hint of a smile ghosting his lips. "Indeed," he said.

With Dahlia and Thorne retreated, the room grew quiet, with only the crackling of the fire in the grate. Their presence had acted as a kind of buffer, dampening Sylvan's intensity. Now that they were gone, Neve found she wasn't sure what to do with her hands, so she clasped them tightly in her lap. Suddenly, Prince Thorne's determination to avoid looking at Dahlia was a very easy thing to understand.

Sylvan eased himself into Thorne's vacated chair. They were brothers, yet opposites in so many ways. Thorne moved like a restless animal, while Sylvan's movements were carefully controlled. As if he planned each one out before committing to it. The firelight cast distorted shadows over the scarred lines of his face, warming the deathly paleness of his skin. He looked... tired. Faint bruises traced beneath his eyes, dark circles threatening to grow even darker.

In all their discussions today, in all their questions, there was one subject that had not arisen. One test that no one had suggested.

"You're going to need to try enthralling me," Neve said.

His gaze snapped up, meeting hers with a brightness that might have been alarm. "No."

She leaned forward. "As a starting point," she said. "We need to know if it feels different. For you. For me."

He was already shaking his head. "Absolutely not."

"It's foolish to ignore the strongest tool we have at our disposal."

He sat with unnatural stillness, his elbow propped on the arm of the chair, fingertips draped over the edge like a boatman reaching out to skim the water. "Most people wouldn't dare call me foolish."

Neve huffed out a breath of frustration. He couldn't refuse

to enthrall her out of principle and then pretend to be a monster. It didn't work that way. "I didn't call you foolish. I said the choice not to try enthrallment was foolish."

Though in this moment, with his storm-gray stare pinning her to her chair, the difference did feel rather slim. Still, she held his gaze as he leaned forward, slowly, and rested his elbows on his knees. Golden sparks stirred in his aura as if awakened from a deep sleep, and her breath stilled in her chest. She had to suppress the urge to reach toward him, to dip her fingers into his aura and see if they would displace the sparks.

She wondered whether he would feel it.

And she wondered, too, when he'd moved so close. His knees were nearly touching hers. Perhaps *she'd* been the one to move.

Still, he held her gaze. No doubt his thoughts were engaged in the serious business of enthrallment and not fixated on the closeness of their bodies. Definitely not recalling that kiss. Or wishing to repeat it.

The room suddenly felt very warm.

"Are you doing it?" she whispered.

"That depends." His voice was a scrape in the dark. "Do you have any inclination to stand up and start dancing a jig?"

She bit back a smile, trying to match his own mock seriousness. "None."

"Then no. Or at least, not effectively."

Neve laughed, and triumph sparked in his eyes, as though that was the greatest possible outcome of this experiment. She was probably misinterpreting it—he probably felt triumphant that the enthrallment hadn't worked, that he could tell her he'd told her so—but even as the thought crossed her mind, she knew it wasn't so.

He liked the fact that he'd made her laugh.

Still, she did what she could to compose herself. "A jig? Really?"

That half smile again. Someday, the man would surrender to that smile, and his entire face would light up. She hoped she'd be there to see it. "I suppose we'll never know."

He sat back in his chair, holding her gaze as if he'd been caught upon it, and she found herself unable to look away. The moment stretched, even as the flecks of gold faded from his aura.

And all at once, the silence was unbearable. Begging to be filled.

"Your powers." The words tumbled out so quickly that she nearly startled herself. "I've seen you work air and iron. I know of the magefire, and the traveling. The poison-speech."

He lifted an eyebrow. "Is there a question in there?"

She cleared her throat. Demons, but she must be even more exhausted than she'd thought. She could barely think straight. "I thought mages wielded two powers at most."

"Three." He dropped his gaze to his hands, and she felt the absence of it like something physical. "The most powerful mages can wield three."

"But you wield more."

"Yes."

"How many?"

His eyes flicked up. "All of them."

"*All* of them," she repeatedly stupidly.

He extended a hand, and the plants on Thorne's mantel sprouted new fist-sized clusters of buds that quickly blossomed into fireworks of red and purple blooms. At the same time, their shadows stretched toward the ceiling, lengthening far longer than the dim light should allow and deepening to near black.

"It's my gift," Sylvan said, voice quiet. "From my extended time in the Miragelands. Every single power wielded by mages. Except for the most important one."

She shook her head, not comprehending. She understood why he despised the poison-speech, but making plants grow was important. Traveling great distances in one step, summoning fire, throwing up shields, commanding the wind… it was a wild combination of powers. He must command dozens, if not hundreds of different abilities.

"What could you possibly be missing?" she asked.

"Healing." This time, his smile was rueful. A far cry from the one she hoped to one day witness. "Perhaps if I'd stayed in that hellscape for another month, I'd have been granted that, too. Or perhaps the Miragelands took me for what I was. Monstrous going in, monstrous coming out. And monsters don't heal people."

She shook her head again, not in confusion this time but in disagreement. He was no monster. Whatever some distant world might or might not have decided.

Questions poured into Neve's mind, each overtaking the next. But she waited, still sitting forward in her chair. He ran his thumb along the arm of his own, almost absently. Almost. Because nothing he did was ever without thought.

"Six years ago," he said, "I was left behind in the Miragelands after the Return. A sandstorm blew in right as the Amethyst Moon ended—that is the window of time we use to make the journey between worlds, when the moon takes on a purple cast here in the Vales—and I lost my vial. I was separated from my group, and Asperion made the call to close the barrier. I was left behind, alone. A death sentence." He cleared his throat, toying with the tassel on the edge of the chair. "It's how my mother died, three years prior to that."

Every three years, a new tragedy. Neve's heart squeezed. "But you didn't."

"Monstrous things thrive in monstrous places."

Three years surviving in the Miragelands, with his supposed father assuming him dead, and his brother… what must it have been like to reunite with them after all that time? With scars beyond the physical ones, the last three years—his return to the Vales—could not have been easy ones.

"I assumed it was a mistake," Sylvan said, "Even in the three years since I've been back, it never once occurred to me that the king would have had the wit, let alone the desire, to leave me for dead. Only now, I think..." He trailed off, expression distant. As if he were recalling every mistake he'd ever made. "Now, I believe Asperion left me behind intentionally. That he wanted to rid himself of his wife's bastard son, in the same way she was lost. Instead, I went in with a single power, a power I detested— poison-speech—and I emerged..." He spread his hands.

With the ability to wield every known power, save for one. It was remarkable. It was also deeply sad. How much had he missed of his world, his brother and his friends, during his absence? She knew what it was not to fit in when you were meant to belong.

No wonder there was a measure of awkwardness between him and the others. They'd grieved his loss, and their lives had moved on. While his had stalled.

"How did you survive?" she asked.

His throat bobbed. "I found a cave system. The dangers are fewer there. I was never quite able to figure out why."

She tried to imagine it. Scraping resources out of a ruined land, so barren that the mages had vacated it centuries ago to invade the Vales. So inundated with monstrous creatures, that they leapt at the chance to believe their king made impossible promises to save them from the need to face it.

Neve had learned long ago that when something sounded too good to be true, it usually was. That Asperion was misleading his people was a given. For what purpose, she didn't know.

Sylvan cleared his throat, leaning forward in his chair and holding her gaze once again, this time with a burning intensity. "If there's anything you know about your immunity, anything you can tell about its origins, then we must know about it. No detail would be too small."

Neve thought of her mother, of the cabin in the woods. Of people coming and going, men and women with knives and rope and fire. Needles sinking into her spine, glass vials filled with liquids as they commanded her to spit, to open, to give of herself again and again and again.

Not one of them had ever learned anything worth knowing.

"Nothing," she said. "There's nothing."

Sylvan nodded, as though it was what he'd expected. "Then we keep working until we find it."

CHAPTER ELEVEN

NEVE

*I*t was three days until the Amethyst Moon—and the Return—and they'd tried everything.

The day after Neve's late-night session with Sylvan, the human servant who'd hurt himself at Asperion's demonstration came hobbling into Thorne's rooms, without knocking, as if he had as much cause to be there as any of them.

And judging by the way the princes leapt out of the way for him—Thorne going so far as to personally fetch a tea service for the man—Neve thought he rather did. He was leaning on a cane, with bandages wrapped up his arms, and he batted even Sylvan away with surprisingly good-natured grunts.

"Can't keep me locked up in that healer's prison forever," he'd groused.

"That *prison* is a top-tier inn for ailing nobility," Sylvan said. "It's run by a couple who have been allies to our cause. They've been helping humans escape the city for years."

Mages, helping humans to flee. A whole network of them. What would Darius and his rebel humans say, if they could hear this conversation? Would they agree to share the Vales with such mages? Or would they throw them behind bars?

The old man had only crossed his arms. "Couple of mother hens, they were. Someone get me a mop. Surely you boys've made a mess or two in my absence."

Sylvan glanced at Neve. "If you want to help us, I've got a better idea."

After determining that Flint—that was the human's name—wasn't under anyone else's thrall and sent to spy on them, they'd set to work.

Neve had tried it all before, attempting to find ways to share her immunity with other humans. Or at least, her mother's frequent visitors had. With Flint's permission, Sylvan enthralled him, his face a mask of displeasure as he did so, while Neve tried to break that enthrallment by holding the old man's hand, by mingling their blood, even by kissing him—a part of the experiment that made Flint blush a bright red, and prompted that rare ghost of a smile from Sylvan.

No matter what they tried, Flint remained enthralled.

Thorne and Dahlia studied the auras, and Sylvan came up with more and more ideas—until Neve was exhausted with giving the man locks of her hair or handkerchiefs from her pockets, whispering instructions in his ear to counter the enthrallment, and waking in the dead of night to try it all again under the light of the waxing moon.

Two days passed, and three, until there were only three nights left before the Return. Flint was dozing by the fire while Thorne leaned against his customary spot at the window and Dahlia lounged on a settee in the corner, a book open in her lap.

As for Sylvan, he paced, his restless energy practically pulsing through the room. Neve got the impression that he tried to mask his emotions behind immovable expressions, but the more time she spent with him, the more she was learning to read his tells. The flutter of tension at the corner of his jaw. The small but conceivable tightening of his eyelids as he considered a problem. The disinterest he attempted to portray when he straightened the cuffs of his shirt.

Most of the time, she found it hard to look away from him.

Now, Neve sat across from Flint for the fourth day in a row. He looked surprisingly peaceful given that they had only three days until the Amethyst Moon, three days until the Return would begin. In another time—a better one—he might have been her grandfather, resting by the fire after a day spent in the gardens. Thorne and Dahlia might be her brother, her sister. And Sylvan… well, Sylvan was a friend.

And if she had to tell herself that last part a little more firmly than the rest, well, she could chalk it up to exhaustion.

In that better time, she'd have embroidery on her lap, her only injuries the pinpricks from her needle—even in her dreams, she could only imagine herself as a poor seamstress—rather than the series of slashes she'd cut into her palms to test her immunity. In a better time, another life? They might all have been enjoying a cozy evening together.

"We're out of options," Thorne said, breaking the illusion with cold, cold reality. And coming from Thorne, who always seemed to be the most cheerful, the most optimistic among them, the proclamation felt especially dire. "We have to do it."

Dahlia shut her book with a clap, though Neve had doubts as to whether she could possibly have been reading it. "Killing the Asp won't solve the problem." Dahlia had taken to shortening the king's name to that of the snake, a practice both princes had embraced with relish. "The mages treat humans so poorly even without him—"

"I'll be king," Thorne interrupted. "I'll stop them."

"It's not that easy. They *need* to be banished."

The vitriol in her words surprised even Neve, but then again, it was impossible to forget the way the other mages had spoken to her in the garden. Even without knowing her secret. Dahlia might speak of symbols and shields, but she hated them as much as Neve did.

"What other options do we have, Dahlia?" Thorne's voice was quiet, but the heat behind it was unmistakable.

And suddenly, the room felt too warm. Too close, as if all the air had been sucked away, her lungs aching for a full breath. Any last feelings of coziness was gone, Thorne and Dahlia's sharp words banishing it like smoke.

Neve stood abruptly. "I'm going for a walk."

She didn't think Thorne and Dahlia even heard her, they were so focused on one another. But she felt Sylvan's eyes tracking her as she practically fled from the room and down the stairs, past the still-empty cages from which she'd released the shimmerlings, and all the way to the landing.

She merely needed a breath of fresh air. Nothing more. If they could work out the next step of the plan in the meantime, so much the better.

As she hurried through the corridor, slippers scuffing on the floor as she headed for the gardens, it was difficult to banish the sensation that she was failing. She'd spent her entire life failing other humans—never able to satisfy their curiosity, never able to pass on her extraordinary gift and save them from the mages —so it honestly shouldn't be all that surprising.

Perhaps it was worse because this time, she actually wanted to help.

Before, she'd chosen selfishness. Unable, and unwilling, to sacrifice more of herself, of her pain, especially when there was nothing she could do to help.

This time was different. And yet it was so very much the same. She was powerless.

Neve darted out of the castle and into the garden, skirts whispering around her legs, and choked in a breath of fresh air. Laced, of course, with the heady scent of lilies and lavender and, curtained along the trellises against the back wall, roses the size of her fist. One breath, and another, and still her heart jerked uneasily against her ribcage, her throat tight with the weight of her failures. She'd been their last hope, and she was letting them down.

Torches burned along the paths, though as she moved further into the gardens, she found the effect was more ominous than cheering. The gardens were silent, though whether it was later than she'd thought or because tonight's festivities were taking place elsewhere, she couldn't say.

Neve followed the path around toward the roses, with half a mind to sink her nose into one and breathe until it filled every sense.

When she reached the black-stone fountain, she let out a startled gasp.

The rebel leader waited beside it as if they'd planned a meeting, hands in his pockets, his long hair tied back with a string. Darius. The one who claimed his ancestors had been kings. How could he possibly have known she was on her way here?

"You've hardly been seen in days," he said, by way of greeting. As if she were late to a conversation he'd already begun. "Are you well?"

Neve pressed a hand to her hair, suddenly aware of how disheveled she must look. She had to bite back a sour response. What did he care about her wellbeing? "I'm fine."

He frowned. "Truly? Locked in the castle with the Soulslayer?"

He didn't put words to his suspicions. He didn't have to. She knew what sacrifice he thought she was making. The Soulslayer's whore, the first hollow he'd ever claimed. The one he thought he'd enthralled.

Neve thought of Sylvan's breath against her lips. *I will not kiss you without your leave.*

"He's not..." She trailed off, grasping for the words that would stem the man's concern. "It's all right."

Darius paced forward, frown deepening as he regarded her over that sharp nose of his. "Demons," he breathed. "You *like* him."

"No," Neve said. Too quickly. Much too quickly. "No. I just... he's not unkind."

Darius came closer still, eyes flashing. "He is a *mage*. Unkindness is in their blood. And you... you may be our only chance."

It was as close as he'd probably ever come to begging in his life. He was a human, as low in status as she was, yet he held himself with such arrogance. As if he knew everything he'd ever need to know. As if he'd never considered changing his mind in anything.

"Steal me away, then," Neve snapped, annoyed. "Kidnap me. Force me. You'll learn nothing. I assure you."

He scoffed. "We leave coercion to *them*."

What if it were different? she wanted to say. *What if there are mages who want to help us?*

But she couldn't trust him with that secret.

Footsteps sounded on the path behind them, and Neve turned toward the sound. When she looked back to the fountain, ready to tell Darius to hide, he was already gone.

Sylvan appeared from behind an overgrown honeysuckle, reaching up to shove its branches aside as they brushed against his jacket. The firelight transformed his hair into a blaze and illuminated the planes of his face, the sharpness of his cheekbones. The deadly beauty that his scars only enhanced. The sight of him made her mouth go dry.

Dear gods. She *did* like him. The thought was a punch to the gut, pushing her already struggling lungs to their limit. What a fool she was.

"There you are." He stopped before her, peering into her face as though reading the page of a particularly interesting novel.

For a moment, she feared he'd see it all, written across her face like a painted sign. Every ridiculous, misguided *feeling*.

If he did, he managed to hide it, for he merely gave her a grim smile. "Our time is up, I'm afraid. Thorne is right. We need to alter our plan."

CHAPTER TWELVE

SYLVAN

*T*he dining room was made of everything Sylvan loathed. Every inch of the space was sharp, shiny, ostentatious—from the red-and-gold checked pattern of the floor to the talon-shaped legs of the clock on the mantel. Sculpted thorns protruded from the dining table and chairs, making his back hurt just to look at them. Even the candlesticks on the table were black, the tapers within them a blood-red crimson.

The servants had laid out a feast of petite fowls and whole fish, fresh oysters rushed in from the coast, and overflowing greens. Chilled wine decanters sweated next to bowls of aggressively ripe fruit—deep green apples and grapes that shone like bruises and oranges so bright they rivaled the flames in the candles.

It was a wonder the table didn't collapse under the weight of the excess.

Sylvan's mother would have hated this. The night of the pre-Return vigil was meant to be one of contemplation, undertaken by the one who would open the magepool. For years, that had been her.

Asperion, of course, had turned it into a party.

The king hadn't yet made an appearance, and the guests milled about in their finery, clutching glasses of wine and laughing a little too loud. The Return was drawing nearer, and despite Asperion's promises, they were on edge.

Sylvan hovered in the corner of the room, glowering at anyone who dared to so much as glance in his direction and doing everything in his power not to check the time obsessively. If Neve and Dahlia were late, or if Thorne failed to stall Asperion, their entire plan would crumble.

Sylvan might be a monster, but this was the first time he'd planned an assassination.

When the doors opened, he barely stopped himself from startling, afraid the king would be the next person to walk through the doors. But Thorne must be succeeding, for it wasn't Asperion who joined them; it was Neve and Dahlia. And Sylvan couldn't help but catch his breath at the sight of them.

Or, more accurately, the sight of *her*.

If the room was all sharpness, then Neve was its opposite. The gown she'd chosen was a deep green color, the silky material clinging tight to her curves, the neckline slashing a deep V between her breasts. The warm tones of her skin were flushed in the candlelight and, as she came closer, he could see that she'd dusted her arms, neck, and chest with speckles of gold.

Proving that gold was not only a hard, sharp thing—but also, under very specific circumstances, soft and alluring. It made him want to drag his tongue along her skin, to fill his ears with the sounds she would make as he licked the gold from the soft spot where her neck met her collarbone.

Neve moved to his side, and he cleared his throat, making an effort to remove his gaze from her chest. "You look the part," he said.

She quirked an eyebrow at him. "I can't tell if that's a compliment or not."

"It isn't." He let his eyes roam her face, taking in the dark swoop of her lashes, the dark red of her lips. "And also, it is."

She gave him a small smile, and it was all he could do not to reach out and touch her hand. It was most assuredly not the time to be distracted by her beauty. But she looked as if she'd just stepped out of a fairytale.

She looked as though she might just be the hero of the damn thing.

"Not all that illuminating, Syl," Dahlia said, striding in behind Neve. Sylvan would have preferred she stay in her rooms tonight, but she'd insisted on attending. Besides, it might well be useful to have her with them. Dahlia's talent was with smoothing shadows, lengthening them and deepening them and, in her more powerful moments, dowsing every light in the room. It was a helpful skill.

Sylvan had it, too. But he expected to be otherwise engaged. Besides, just because he had access to every known kind of magic did not mean he was a master of them all. Even weakened by her half-human blood, Dahlia's mastery of shadow work was superior to his.

The door opened again, and King Asperion appeared, his cheeks ruddy, as though he was already well into his imbibing for the evening. Though the evening was warm, he wore a fur stole over his shoulders, the edges dyed a garish red.

In his arms, he carried the cask full of donated magepool water.

As soon as the king entered, Neve moved closer to Sylvan. And then, to his utmost surprise, she draped herself against his side, sliding one arm around his waist. The move so shocking that he nearly stepped away from her.

But one look at her face, the flicker of exasperation at the way he'd tensed beneath her touch, and he understood. Fool that he was. She was merely playing her role.

And that role didn't leave a sliver of space between them.

A ruse, only. Even through the fabric of their clothes, he could feel the heat of her, the softness of her curves as she pressed herself to his side. The feel of her against him reignited everything he'd felt during that kiss. A full week ago, and still it distracted his mind.

An understatement, if there ever was one. Distracted? No, it *dominated*.

Swallowing, he willed his body to calm the fuck down. Even as he curled an arm around her waist, adjusting his belt so that his vial was at the front of his hip instead of his side, so that he could pull her closer still. The softness of the silk between his fingers, and the warmth of her skin beneath it, nearly undid him.

Sylvan had a brief, visceral image of sweeping everything off the table and laying her down upon it. Of running his hands up her thighs, of tasting every part of her.

Thorne entered behind Asperion, and Sylvan forced himself to set the image aside. Utter foolishness. Every touch between them was a performance; he would do well to remember it. Even if his body very clearly did not.

Asperion, who'd been making the rounds to the other guests, paused in front of Sylvan. "Haven't tired of your human toy yet eh, Sylvan?" Asperion winked at Neve, and though Sylvan could feel her trembling—whether with fear or rage or both, he couldn't say—she kept her face entirely blank.

She'd spent a long time pretending to be enthralled. A lifetime. And here Sylvan prided himself on keeping his emotions in check. She was a revelation.

"I'm sure that you, of all people, are glad to miss this year's Return," Asperion said, his focus now fully on Sylvan. "I hope this will provide you with some relief."

Relief. As though Sylvan had ever shown an ounce of weakness in front of this man.

But even as the thought crossed his mind, he couldn't

pretend he'd been all that careful in the way he'd acted around the king. He'd underestimated the Asp; he would not do so again.

The king was waiting for a reply. And so Sylvan reached out a hand. "Indeed."

The king nodded, jovial as ever, and moved on to speak to the next guest, Thorne following with a wide smile and that too-loud laugh that he had no idea betrayed his nerves.

No matter. Asperion was here. Thorne was here. It was time to put their plan into motion.

Sylvan took Neve's hand in his, leading her out toward the veranda. At least no one at the party was likely to question why they were stepping out. Or why they were leaving the more brightly lit parts of the grounds in favor of the shadows.

Sylvan led Neve back around into the fortress and through the quiet hallways toward the throne room, where one of the tower stairwells held another secret. He bent to dislodge a loose stone from the floor, revealing a narrow stone staircase.

"Thorne and Asperion won't enter from here," he said. "They'll come through the garden entrance."

"Hard to imagine Asperion navigating this," she said, picking her way along the steps with care.

"Indeed."

The staircase dumped them out into a musty underground passage. He hadn't quite known how to prepare her for this. It wasn't just an underground passage, not just a storage chamber or even a crypt.

The walls were shaped into low shelves, as if they'd once been benches, and the remains of a stone table sat forgotten in the corner, the edges rounded with age.

Neve brushed a hand along the wall, her fingertips pausing before the remains of a brightly painted fresco. He'd never been able to make out the figures; people, perhaps gathered around a fire.

"What is this place?" she asked.

Sylvan dragged his gaze away from her. "The human castle. From before the mages."

He watched understanding flicker across her face, her skin blanching as she took in the details with new eyes. Holes in the walls lined in rust might once have held candle sconces. The broken tiles on the floor might have been a colorful mosaic. There might have been music, and light.

It might have been beautiful, once. Before the mages and their destruction. Now, it was nothing but ruins.

"So the king keeps his vigil down here before the Return," Neve said. "Not very pleasant, is it?"

Only if you wanted to relive the horrors of the past. "Technically, it's meant to be Thorne's vigil. His blood opens the mage-pool, not Asperion's. But the king insists on accompanying him, as he did our mother."

Her eyebrows lifted. "She used to be the one to open the pool?"

He nodded. "Blood from the royal line of the mages opens the pool."

"Who decides these things, anyway?" she muttered. "You're royal, you're not. Your blood opens a portal to another realm. Your blood does not. It's exhausting."

Sylvan suppressed a laugh. "I've never thought of it that way." He ran a finger along the edge of the frescos. "Only... if the land were to choose someone to be a queen, it was right that it should have been her. She wanted to change things."

His mother had always approached the task of opening the pool with a mixture of reverence and pure, delighted excitement. "She would prick her finger with a sewing needle and hold it out over the pool, so certain..." He shook his head, as if he could shake the memory of her face from his mind. "So hopeful that things would be different this time. It's one of my earliest memories. Seeing her hold her hand out like that, hope beaming across her face. Like perhaps the Miragelands would be ready to welcome us home."

She'd never even lived there. None of them had, not for three hundred years.

"But it never did."

"I think she believed that if the Miragelands were miraculously healed, made livable again, that we'd all return there and leave the humans alone. She taught us that it was wrong. The way humans are treated."

Neve was standing so still, it was impossible to gauge her feelings. She must hate him, for what his people had done. "And what do you think?"

He shook his head. "I think the mages are too obsessed with power. I think they—*we*—would have found a way to wrench the gates open and lord over both places." He kicked at the floor, rubbing at a nonexistent scuff. "But it never happened, anyway. The Miragelands are as ruined as they ever were."

And in the end, the Miragelands had claimed his mother. Just as they'd tried to claim him.

It had been a long time since he'd allowed himself to think of her. A longer time still since he'd spoken to anyone of her, Thorne included. He and his brother buried their grief, working through it in different ways. Thorne pushed it outward, seeking physical comfort, spending physical energy, whenever he was able. With women, with sword training.

Sylvan's had been left within his chest to rot.

Neve looked like she would ask another question, but Sylvan extended a hand, wrapping her fingers once again in his. "They'll be here shortly."

They hid themselves in a half-collapsed alcove, the entrance obscured by the crumbling remains of a stone column. He'd scouted the area ahead of time, knowing that Thorne and Asperion would enter the ruins from the other direction. It would give them a good line of sight while hopefully keeping them well out of the way. Until the time was right.

Once inside, though, the alcove was tighter than it had looked. Neve inched in beside him, nearly as close as she'd been at the party. But a sliver of torchlight still illuminated the corner of her dress, and he feared it would make her visible from the passage.

Sylvan leaned back against the wall, pulling her forward so that she was squeezed into the space between him and the column. Her breasts were flush against his chest, and his body was all too aware of every curve in hers. Her legs wedged between his knees. The pulsing vein in her throat fluttering rapidly.

Before he could stop himself, he reached up to brush a strand of hair away from her cheek. His gaze fell to her mouth as she licked her bottom lip, his focus utterly forgotten.

"Sylvan," she breathed.

Voices echoed from down the corridor, and he pressed a finger to her lips. A bad idea. A very bad idea. Her lips were soft, her breath warm against his skin. Gods take him, but he wanted nothing more than to see her draw that finger into her mouth.

"...sure it's the best course of action to leave the guards behind tonight," Asperion was saying. "What with the attempts on your life."

"Surely we can handle ourselves, Father," Thorne's voice replied. "It's tradition to perform the vigil alone."

To someone who didn't know him as thoroughly as Sylvan, his tone might have passed as casual. To Sylvan, though, the words sounded too quick. Too loud.

Their shadows interrupted the flickering light of the torch as they stopped in what had once been the seat of the humans' power. Sylvan dropped his lips to Neve's ear. "Stay here."

He slid out from behind the column.

And Neve followed, ignoring his instruction and instead

sticking close to his side. He wanted to curse her, but there was no time.

The plan hinged on surprise.

Sylvan launched himself at the king, covering the distance quickly. Without pausing to take in the king's surprise, he closed his hands around Asperion's throat.

The king still carried the cask, but it was no matter; he could feel the Asp's blood thrumming within him, his power. Sylvan reached, delving deep, as he had with the would-be assassin. Feeling past the layers of skin and flesh to the bone, to the marrow that beat at the heart of the king's body. He reached for his magefire—

And the world *shifted*.

His magic stopped.

His magic. Why had he been using his magic? Against the king? His thoughts were confused, the dust of the underground suddenly clustering in his nostrils. The king had taken him in, had been as a father to him despite the questions about his paternity. Despite the way his mother had betrayed him. Why would Sylvan use his powers *against* him?

Sylvan shook his head, trying to clear his thoughts. He could feel Neve's gaze on him, the question in her eyes as he clasped Asperion's throat. She must be horrified.

He tried to loosen his fingers, to remove them from the king's throat, but somehow, they wouldn't move. As inaccessible to his commands as his magic.

His chest tightened, a sense of wrongness pulling at his ribs.

"I *was* curious how you would attempt it," Asperion said. "Poison in the cup? A knife to the back?" The king withdrew with a jerk, wiping a hand across his neck as though to dispel a clump of dirt. Perhaps Sylvan's hands *had* been dirty. Though, he remembered bathing before he arrived. His hands were still outstretched, fingers frozen in claw-like curves.

The king pressed his index finger into Sylvan's chin, pushing his head up at an awkward angle. "I ought to have known you wouldn't be able to resist the chance to flaunt your powers. *Son.*"

A trickle of awareness cut a pathway through his mind. And with a wave of nausea, Sylvan understood.

It should be impossible—it *was* impossible—but Asperion had him enthralled. Under his control. Sylvan couldn't access his own magic.

He was powerless.

Asperion released Sylvan's chin. "I control your magic now, boy."

CHAPTER THIRTEEN

NEVE

*N*eve hadn't known Sylvan for long—days, only—yet she knew he would never allow anyone to touch him that way. Yet King Asperion had his fingernail jammed into the flesh of the Soulslayer's chin, and Sylvan did nothing.

He didn't move. He didn't unleash his powers. He didn't even speak.

He just let it happen.

Fear coiled through her gut, sharp and hot, even before the king put words to what she'd already known. "I control your magic now, boy."

Neve stopped breathing. Mages couldn't be enthralled. Everyone knew that. She might have taken it for years of lies, only Sylvan had confirmed it. And whatever else he might be, he wasn't a liar. Not to her.

Mages couldn't be enthralled, and yet—and yet, Sylvan *was*. As fully and completely as Flint had been before he'd slashed his own wrists. As fully and completely as *she* was supposed to be. His body, still pressed close against hers, was stiff and unmoveable, his fingers still stretched before him as if to claw at the king's throat.

Enthrallment over humans was horrific enough. But control over the Soulslayer meant control over his abilities. The most powerful mage in generations, and the king had managed to grasp hold of his magic.

But how was Asp accomplishing it? He'd boasted of his experimental approach to magic, his acumen with developing new uses for their powers. But never had she imagined he might turn those experiments against the mages themselves. What could he possibly want from this?

Neve stayed still, her mind racing as she hoped, against everything, that she could come up with a plan before Asperion remembered she existed. As she hoped, too, that she was too small, too inconsequential, for the king to notice. Just a human. Just a nobody.

A fool's hope, as Asperion turned his gaze on her, eyes raking down her body. "Maybe I'll take your whore right here on this floor while you watch," he said. "She's pretty enough, for a hollow. Should I release her enthrallment just enough so she knows what's happening? Remind her exactly what she is, on the ruins of her ancestors?"

Sylvan's arm trembled as he fought the enthrallment. But he didn't reply. Thorne, too, was silent; Neve could only assume it meant that he had also been captured in Asperion's thrall.

The king rolled his eyes and huffed out a breath. "You may speak. More satisfying that way."

Sylvan's breath was a rasp in his throat, loud next to her ear. "I'll kill you."

Asperion moved closer to Neve, eyes sparkling with triumph. She could smell spiced meat on his breath, along with the bite of red wine. "You tried to, didn't you? Not good enough, as usual." He pressed a fingertip to Neve's upper arm, dragging it down toward her elbow, tongue wedged between his teeth as if he were imagining the taste of her. She barely restrained a shudder. "I knew you liked her, you know. You thought you were so clever. That I wouldn't notice the difference in your servants. The spring in their steps. Never in thrall."

A smile curled his lips. "And now this woman. Never in thrall either. At least, not until now."

His aura was practically throbbing with magic, the sparks trilling outward toward her, toward Sylvan. And toward the cask.

But no; as she watched, it became clear that the sparks were trailing *out* of the cask. Before the demonstration, he'd claimed to have collected drops of magepool water from all the mages who were present. Asperion had claimed he could use them to restore his people's magic on his own—that if they trusted him, they would have no need to face the horrors of the Miragelands.

If the drops could create such a connection to their magic, then that connection could also be exploited. That must be how he was enthralling them now.

That must be his true intention.

"Father," Thorne said, his voice tight. He was standing too far behind her for Neve to see his face without turning her head, which would give away the only advantage they had. If only she could figure out how to exploit it.

Asperion dropped his hand, stepping away from Neve and turning to face Thorne. "My true son. And a true disappointment. How many lives *do* you have?"

A moment. She had no more than a moment. "The cask," she breathed. "He's using the connection to control you."

"My vial," Sylvan whispered. "Your blood."

Her blood had never helped humans to escape enthrallment. Not once. And oh, how she had bled over the years in service of that discovery.

But humans weren't bound by the magepool, and Sylvan was not a human.

It might not work. But there would be no knowing, unless they tried.

Slowly, Neve dropped her hand to Sylvan's hip and the flask of magepool water he kept there. She fumbled with the cork, using two fingers to ease it out. She could feel Sylvan's tension, and it made her want to hurry. But this couldn't be rushed.

"It was you," Thorne said. "The assassination attempts."

Asperion waved the question away, like it was a fly disturbing his peace. Like its very existence was a bore. "Yes, yes. A clean slate. Don't look so hurt, boy. Don't act like you haven't held me in contempt all your life. I blame your poisonous bitch of a mother. Though if I'd noticed her determination to influence your mind sooner, I might have been able to intervene."

Balancing the cork between two fingers, Neve sliced open the freshly healed cut on her palm. She dragged her skin across the lip of Sylvan's vial, not daring to look down, to watch the drops hit the water. She hardly dared to breathe.

If this didn't work, they'd be dead within minutes. She didn't see what she could do to stop it. Not on her own.

Warmth bloomed up Sylvan's arm, and he stepped away from her, magefire blooming from his fingertips.

Free. Her blood had *freed* him. She nearly staggered with the relief of it.

Asperion rounded on Sylvan, shock painted across his face, and then he was meeting Sylvan's magefire with a blast of his own. Thorne's magefire, perhaps, or that of another mage. There'd been so many of them at the party. Was he already controlling them all?

Neve dashed for Thorne, wrenching open the vial at his neck and scraping her blood into it.

"I could kiss you," he said. "Only I expect my brother might object."

A band of black shadows blew into the room, and Dahlia

appeared from the same stairwell Neve and Sylvan had used to get down here.

She was beautiful, dark hair melting into the shadows as if they were one and the same. Her appearance gave Sylvan the upper hand, and he blasted Asperion back against the nearest wall.

And then Sylvan was grabbing Neve's arms, looking into her eyes with wild intensity. "Is there anything that could help us understand," he said, breathing hard. "Anyone who might know more about your powers. Anyone at all?"

Powers. She'd never thought about her immunity that way.

Neve let out a breath. It was unlikely, and she didn't want to, but there was no choice. "My mother," she said. "She lives in Sprye Village."

Sylvan dove for Thorne, who was already clasping Dahlia's hand. Together, they twisted away.

CHAPTER FOURTEEN

SYLVAN

They landed in the middle of a dirt road. Though the moon was almost full—the Amethyst Moon nearly upon them—it was obscured by a thick band of clouds, making it too dark to see more than a few paces in any direction.

Sylvan risked lighting an orb of magefire, lifting it high so he could take in their surroundings. Narrow buildings slouched to either side, made from a mishmash of wood and stone, most with only open slits for windows. It was, as far as he could tell, like any other village: rickety porches, small squared-off gardens, the unmistakable smell of horses.

"Where?" he said, turning around as though he could guess where Neve's mother resided simply by surveying the buildings. "Where is she?"

His body was shaking as though he'd caught a chill, the magefire trembling above his palm. He tried to force it to stop, to hold himself still, but it was as if his mind had lost control of his body. As if Asperion were still standing before him, holding him in thrall.

"A moment of respite, brother." Thorne was bent over, his

hands pressed to his knees. He looked like he might be sick. "We need a moment."

Sylvan ripped his vial from his belt and poured the blood-stained water into the dirt. "We don't have a moment. You and Dahlia need to get horses. Go tell Jessa and Kael and the others to spread the word that everyone must take off their vials."

Thorne nodded, following Sylvan's lead and removing the vial of magepool water he wore around his neck. He offered his hand to Dahlia, and she accepted it, the two of them hurrying to find the stables together.

Neve stood in the center of the street, staring at the rickety collection of wooden buildings with an expression that fell somewhere between dread and resignation. The distant expression looked wrong on her face; she was a person who took interest in everything, who stood her ground, who released shimmerlings and stuck her nose into oversized flowers and partnered with people who ought to be her enemies. She was a person who noticed *everything*.

Sylvan forced himself to take a breath, and then another. He had to calm himself, for her sake if nothing else. After a few breaths, the shaking began to taper off, though it didn't cease entirely.

Neve had led Sylvan to believe her mother had died, had accepted his condolences on her loss. He'd spent the last few days assuming she was alone in the world, with no one to protect her. With no family.

He wasn't angry, precisely. It was more... confusion, really, than anything else. He hadn't anticipated the deception, and he wasn't sure what to make of it. But it didn't matter. They were here now; they would talk to Neve's mother, and learn what they could. Assuming it wasn't too late.

"She lives outside the village," Neve said. "You're right. We should go."

But Sylvan's pounding heart was beginning to slow, the

world coming into clearer focus as his panic ebbed. Time was short, but it wasn't gone. "Thorne's right," he said. "We can take a moment."

She didn't respond.

Sylvan's usual idea of bedside manner was to stay as far away from said bedside as possible. Dahlia was better suited for such tasks. Even Thorne would be preferable. They were people who knew what to say. How to help.

Sylvan was more likely to slap someone on the arm and demand they snap out of it than he was to offer tea and sympathy.

He didn't expect that approach would be very helpful at the moment. And Neve clearly needed *something*. "Are you all right?" he asked. The words still came out clipped, almost as bad as the slap would have been. As if he were accusing her of *not* being all right.

He cleared his throat, intending to try again, but Neve said, "I'm fine."

Her lips barely moved, her voice barely audible. And somehow, this seemingly invulnerable woman looked... lost.

"You saved us back there." He cleared his throat again. "You saved me. Thank you."

She only nodded.

What had happened to her here, to so thoroughly drain her of all her vivacity, all her nerve? How many humans had she seen enthralled, with no way to help them? It must have been lonely, at the very least. Perhaps she'd left here to protect her mother, and everyone else she cared about.

He'd known enthrallment was horrible, had always hated the very idea of it. The fact that mages could do it at all seemed a serious mark against their race as a whole. His mother had believed it was meant to be a different power altogether—something the mages had corrupted and used for ill gains once they arrived in the Vales. *Perhaps we once used our minds to speak with animals,* she'd said. *Perhaps in the Miragelands, we used even this magic for good.*

He'd wanted to believe that. But it had become increasingly difficult over the years, as he'd witnessed all the terrible things his people did with the power. Hard to imagine them using it for softer pursuits.

And watching others subjected to enthrallment, even as he planned to end it forever, was nothing to the feeling of enduring it.

Thanks to Neve, Sylvan had only endured Asp's thrall for a few minutes. But it made his skin crawl to think of the way the king had twisted his wishes and fogged his mind. It had been worse still when Asp had allowed him back into his own thoughts while leaving him unable to move. Unable to help protect Neve or help his brother. Utterly powerless.

Sylvan had never considered that there might be a way for a mage to be compelled in this manner. The idea of Asp controlling anyone's powers was sobering. But the idea of him controlling Sylvan's cut a chill straight to his marrow. With his powers and a lack of any conscience whatsoever, the king would have been unstoppable.

Before Sylvan could decide whether to voice any of this, or what to say next, Neve gave herself a shake. As if in a dream, she started toward the edge of the village.

Sylvan followed, keeping the orb of magefire alight in his palm. It had steadied somewhat, and it illuminated the path before them in strands of blue and purple, allowing them to walk without stumbling. Still, every rustle from the underbrush made his heart leap, his equanimity crumbling as if Asperion's delving into his mind had broken some critical part of him. As if he'd been cracked wide open. All his weaknesses revealed.

After about a mile, they reached a cottage.

Sylvan couldn't help but feel like a child in a fairytale as Neve paused at the end of the walkway. He let the magefire fade, forcing himself to draw a long, slow breath. "Is this the place?"

Neve swallowed.

Sylvan stepped closer to her, breathing in that herbal scent she carried with her everywhere. "We don't have to do this. We'll find another way."

They *did* have to do it. There *wasn't* another way. But looking at her face, drawn and almost pinched as though she were in pain, he wanted it to be true. Desperately.

Then it was too late as the cottage door swung open, and a woman appeared. She held a lantern above her head, squinting out into the night. Her figure was tall and willowy, her long hair hanging loose around her shoulders.

As soon as she saw them, her face split into a grin. And then she was running down the path to greet them, throwing her arms around Neve, who allowed herself to be embraced without returning the gesture. Like a doll, gathered into the overenthusiastic arms of a child.

"The sprites were right!" the woman cried. "They told me you were on your way. 'Ava,' they said, 'your girl is coming home.' So I whipped up an apple blackberry pie, quick as you like. And here you are!"

Sylvan looked at Neve, eyebrows raised. "Sprites?"

He'd never heard of such a creature existing in the Vales. Or in the Miragelands, come to that. They belonged in fairy stories, and that was all.

Neve's mother released the hug, still gripping her daughter's shoulders. It didn't seem possible, but her eyes widened even further, her smile stretching to impossible lengths as her gaze landed on Sylvan. "Oh, my land! You've brought a suitor."

As though he were a normal man, and not an enemy mage. Not the dreaded Soulslayer. Just another suitor. One of many, perhaps.

She patted her hair, as if Neve had brought the suitor for *her*.

"Come in, come in. I'm Ava. But then, I'm sure you know that. Neve would have told you all about her eccentric mother, I've no doubt."

Ava hurried forward, the lantern held aloft. Sylvan followed, sticking close to Neve's side. He had the sudden urge to wrap an arm around her waist, to shield her from whatever was about to happen. "Does she not know who I am?" he asked quietly.

"The village is three days ride from Vunmore. I'd never seen your face before I came there, either. She wouldn't recognize you."

Sylvan hesitated, wondering if Neve's mother was entirely well. "And the sprites?"

Neve cringed. "One of her fancies. I don't know if she believes in them, really. But she puts on a good show for her customers."

Sylvan started to ask what she meant, but Neve shook her head before he could voice the question. "You'll see."

As soon as they crossed the threshold, he did.

The room was packed, from floor to ceiling, with fortune-telling accoutrements. An assortment of glass spheres sat in a line on the floor along one wall, ranging from the size of his thumbnail to that of his skull. The shelf in the corner was stacked with cards, some hand drawn, others painted in meticulous detail. Gauzy material hung from the walls, dyed in purples and greens and blues and no doubt meant to look sumptuous—except that the streaks and lines suggested poor technique, poor materials, or both.

It *did* smell like pie, though.

Ava set two plates on the table, so quickly that Sylvan did wonder if she might be gifted with a hint of future-casting, however small. He'd never heard of such a thing in a human—or, truthfully, in a mage—but if nothing else, everything he'd endured had shown him that the limits of magic and powers were practically unfathomable.

Neve didn't trust her; that much was clear. And so Sylvan, too, proceeded with caution as he sat at the table beside Neve.

"Charlie came by yesterday, Neve," Ava said. "You wouldn't even believe how skinny the man's gotten. I keep telling him to go see a healer, but you know how he is. Stubborn to the last."

She spoke as though Neve had gone away for a brief holiday, or even to the store for a loaf of bread.

"I'm sorry," Sylvan said. "I just—I'd thought it had been a long time since you'd seen one another."

Ava gave Neve's wrist a playful tap. "It's been five years! Five *years*, you mischievous thing."

Sylvan might not know much, but he knew something about family bonds. And he knew that if Thorne had gone missing for five years, he'd have stopped at nothing until he found his brother. He'd have ripped the entire country apart in search of him.

He wouldn't be smiling and relaxed, baking pies and talking to imaginary sprites.

Neve said nothing.

Not like her. Not like her at all.

"But you're back now," Ava said. "Your suitor here will see."

Neve didn't even argue with the suitor assumption. And it wasn't lost on Sylvan that Ava had not bothered to ask his name.

Ava leaned toward Sylvan, her green eyes alight. How they could be so like Neve's and so unlike them at the same time, Sylvan didn't understand. She made a move as though to take his hands, but when he didn't reach for her, she placed her outstretched palms on the table. "Neve's blood is incredibly special. She cannot be enthralled by the mages. It's extraordinary."

Sylvan couldn't help it. He stared at her. "That," he said, "is a secret that could get your daughter killed. And you think nothing of revealing it to a stranger."

At that, Neve's mother actually laughed. "Keep it secret?
When there's not a human alive who wouldn't give everything
they have to learn how it's done? You should *see* how much they
pay. When Neve isn't being churlish and selfish about it, that
is."

Sylvan's heart skittered in his chest. Surely he could not have
heard that right. "You sell her blood?"

"Blood," Neve repeated dully. "Saliva. Locks of hair. Patches
of skin, shaved in little squares. Or strips, sometimes."

No fucking wonder Neve hadn't wanted to come here.
Sylvan ground his teeth. "Do you know why Neve has this
immunity?"

"The sprites, of course." Ava said it so matter-of-factly, as if it
were the most obvious thing in the world. "They favor her."

Nausea clawed at Sylvan's gut, and he pushed it down,
focusing on Ava. The sooner they could get answers from her,
the sooner they could be gone. "Her father, then. Who... where
is he?"

"Gone," Neve whispered.

Ava pressed a hand to her chest. "Rest his soul. Gone near
twenty years now. The fool used to spin tall tales. Always said
he was born to be King of Silerith. Can you imagine?"

Sylvan couldn't. His first thought was that the man must
have been just as delusional as his wife. Silerith. That had been
one of the human nations, long ago.

Neve, though, looked up abruptly. "What did you say?"

"It's nothing darling, really." Ava fluttered her fingers, rings
flashing in the candlelight. "I wouldn't have you chasing
fancies."

Not like the very real chasing of sprites.

"What did he say about the King of Silerith?" Neve asked
quietly.

Ava sighed. "It was all nonsense. He said his great-great-
great grandparents ruled over the northern country long ago.

Silerith. But who doesn't want to believe they're descended of kings? Trust me." She patted the crystal ball in the center of the table. "I work a good trade, telling them what they want to hear. Someone did the same for your father, I've no doubt. He never would let it go."

Neve stood. Without another word, she turned and headed for the door.

"Where are you going?" Ava pushed her chair back, though she didn't bother to stand. "What—"

Sylvan rose from his chair, waiting until Neve had passed through the door before leaning over her still-seated mother. When he had her attention, he called a plume of magefire back to his palm, reveling in the way the color drained from the woman's face. "If I could be sure Neve wanted it," he said, "I would burn you to ash right here."

With that, he followed Neve into the night.

CHAPTER FIFTEEN

NEVE

*R*ain pelted Neve's face as she fled the cottage she'd never been comfortable calling a home, the stinging sweetness of the pie still burning in the back of her nostrils. The clouds had broken open in earnest, but nothing short of an impossible compulsion would have kept her inside those walls. She was drenched in seconds, her flimsy dress sucking tight against her skin and nearly tripping her up as she ran. Without slowing, she grabbed the fabric and hiked it up over her hips until her legs were free, kicking off her restrictive shoes to run barefoot back toward the village.

Leave it to her mother not to even comment on the gown. She'd hardly seemed to notice Neve's absence, so it wasn't likely that she'd notice the expensive fabric and dye, or the low cut of the neckline.

Though perhaps the richness of it had inspired her to charm Sylvan in hopes of gaining access to his wallet. The woman was adept at charming everyone she met, from the village baker to the constable who'd once side-eyed her business, to the clients who waltzed regularly through her door and relied on her false fortunes to make momentous decisions in their lives. She was loved by all, when she ought to be trusted by none.

Except... except that she *hadn't* appeared to charm Sylvan. In fact, he'd only seemed to become more enraged by every word she uttered. His face might not have betrayed it, but the way he'd pressed his fingertips together until the skin beneath his nails turned white... he hadn't enjoyed the conversation. At all.

He caught up with her now, his expression as dark as the storm itself. She realized she was crying, hot tears glazing her cheeks beneath the chill of the rain. She couldn't stop the violent shivers of her shoulders, the clatter of her teeth. Out here it was cold, and wet, and still infinitely better than the inside of her mother's cottage.

Should he try to convince her to return, she would sit down right here. She'd rather perish of cold than go back, and if that made her melodramatic, well, she'd earned the right. Whether he believed it or not.

Sylvan took hold of her arm, pulling her close against his side. He was as drenched as she, yet standing close to him... it felt like leaning close to warm her hands by a fire, like the comfortable feeling that settled in her chest while drinking tea in Lydia's shop after hours. It should have felt like danger. Instead it felt like... safety. Like home, in a way that stuffed-to-the-eaves cottage never had. Never could.

Blearily, she tried to shake off the sensation. Sylvan Everstone was not a home. The Soulslayer was not a comfort. He was a means to an end, a temporary friend. A reluctant ally whose desires were briefly aligned with hers.

But as he led her into the village, practically lifting her up the steps to the inn when they reached it, she found herself unable to fully believe any of that. The Sylvan the world saw bore little resemblance to the man who walked at her side now.

The old man behind the bar at the inn leapt to attention when Sylvan strode in, half carrying Neve. Even in her distress, she could tell the proprietor would have granted them whatever they wished regardless of the heavy purse Sylvan dropped on the counter. He led them to a large guest room, the hearth already lit—perhaps in anticipation of another, less frightening guest—and answered Sylvan's demand for blankets quickly before practically fleeing. Likely to hide back behind his counter.

The blankets were simple, but they were clean. As she stripped the ruined silk from her body to wrap them around her, Sylvan turning his back to allow her a semblance of privacy, she thought they might be the very best thing she'd ever felt. Scratchy wool notwithstanding.

She took her time securing the blankets, draping a second over her shoulders and shaking her wet hair out to dry. Her hands were shaking, less from the cold now than from the need to tell the story. The whole story, the whole truth. To the man she ought to have confessed it to long before this.

He was still facing the door. She didn't have to look him in the eye, at least.

"She sold my time," she said. She had to say it, now, before the words festered inside any longer.

He turned slowly, as if to give her time to order him to look away. She didn't, and he faced her, meeting her eyes with an intensity that tightened her chest. Not with anxiety, but with pure, unfiltered *want*.

The anger in his eyes was on her behalf. She knew it, like she knew that he wanted to *protect* her. To intervene on her behalf, where no one ever had.

In a way, she felt as if she was seeing him clearly for the first time.

"They bled me," she went on, throat dry. "Poked me. Tested whatever they could test. Sometimes… sometimes, I don't know if they even really believed in my immunity at all. Or if they just wanted to…" She held out her hands, helpless to describe what she meant. Some men just enjoyed causing harm to others. Some women, too.

His throat bobbed. "Did they... did any man—"

Neve shook her head. But the answer wasn't exactly a joyous one. "They would have. I got old enough that I think she'd have whored me out to them without hesitation, if it meant extra coin. That was why I ran."

Sylvan moved away from the door, running his long fingers through his hair. The wet locks fell around his pale skin like fire consuming a match. She watched him, transfixed, as he came toward her. She thought he would sit on the edge of the bed, or move to the chair, but he stopped just short of where she stood, looking into her face as if scanning for injuries. "I'm sorry I subjected you to that."

As though she hadn't told him of her mother's existence herself. As if she hadn't been the one to bring them there. Her throat burned. Close as he was, he wasn't even touching her, probably hadn't once considered doing so—outside of their ruse, that was—yet her entire body seemed to be catching on fire.

"And for no gain," he went on, oblivious to the inferno that raged within her. "We're out of time and we learned nothing."

Neve adjusted the blanket on her shoulders. In a moment, when she told him the truth, his protectiveness would give way to anger *at* her, rather than on her behalf. She wanted to put it off. To keep the light in his eyes shining for her. But wouldn't that make her the selfish creature her mother always claimed her to be?

"We did learn something," she admitted.

Sylvan frowned, giving his head a small shake, and she pulled the blanket tighter, as if it might be her shield. "You'll kill me, if I tell you." He sucked in a breath, ready to deny it, but she said, "You have to promise you won't."

He looked at her for a long, long moment, jaw working

soundlessly. But his mastery over his own expression had never been more complete. Whether he was contemplating an 'it depends' or a 'how dare you,' she couldn't have said.

Finally, he nodded. If nothing else, he knew his reputation. And he knew exactly how much of it must have been earned. "You're safe with me, Neve. You have my word."

His voice was a rasp in the dark, her name like a sacred oath. And she wanted to believe him. She hoped this wasn't a mistake. Though if it was, well, maybe she deserved it. For running away. For failing to help those stuck under enthrallment.

"I met another human," she said softly. "A rebel. He came to me to ask for help in a rebellion against the mages."

Sylvan let out a breath. And then, to her utter shock, he gave her a small smile. As if he meant to be encouraging. "It's no surprise to learn there are rebels among the humans. Nor that they'd want to work with someone who'd risen to your... status."

But that was not the secret she feared would enrage him. She didn't return his smile. Nor did she wish to see his fade to disappointment.

"Darius is like me," she said. "He can't be enthralled. Sylvan, he claims to be descended of kings."

Sylvan was quiet. And indeed, the smile had faded from his lips. She mourned it.

"I never heard this tale from my father," she went on, hurrying now. "What my mother said about Silerith. But if Darius and I are both descended from these royal lines..."

"Then maybe your Vales blood can shut the magepool. Just as Thorne's royal mage blood can open it."

Something like that. The tears had returned now, along with the shivers. "I'm sorry," she said. "I should have told you."

Sylvan raised his hand and cupped her face, slowly brushing her tears away with his thumb. "You didn't know if you could trust me. You were protecting them."

Was she? Or was she protecting herself? "If I wasn't so self-ish, I might have figured it out before."

"Selfish?" For the first time, his tone was harsh, though his thumb was still warm on her cheek, her skin tingling in every place he touched her. "I cannot imagine something more selfless than letting us poke and prod and test you like that, after all you endured. You should have said something."

Her breath caught in her throat, coming out as a sob. "It was on my terms."

And it was. It had been. She might not have trusted Sylvan—or Thorne, or even Dahlia—but everything they'd done had been on her terms. She'd not considered declaring any test too invasive, but if she had done, they'd have discontinued it without question. She knew that, just as she knew that this man, this mage with his utterly cruel reputation, was standing before her regretting it all because of the hurt it *might* have caused.

She leaned into his hand, and his fingers stilled, his breath catching audibly in his throat. "I want to kiss you," he said, his words warming the air between them. "On your terms."

I will not kiss you without your leave. How was it that no one knew of this man's kindness? Of his deep-seated desire to do good, to make the world a better place? Revenge on his own behalf hadn't even factored into his plans to free the Vales. He hadn't known, until a few days ago, that it should.

"Yes," she breathed.

This kiss was not at all like their first.

Their first, the supposed ruse, had been all heat, all pressure, all desperate urges mixed with fear and confusion and want, the memory of blood hanging thick in the air.

When Sylvan lowered his lips to hers now, he did it slowly. Deliberately. With the same care he took in all his movements, all his expressions. Only now, he focused it entirely on her. On the torturous swipe of his tongue along her upper lip, the press of his hand to the back of her neck, the slow swirl of his finger as he caressed the place where her hairline met her spine. Electricity vaulted through her body as he dropped a hand to her hip, even though her skin was buried beneath layers of blanket.

Sensations cascaded through her like snow flurries, each passing through before making room for the next just to come back around again—the heat of his mouth on hers, the soft exhale of his breath between kisses, the thoroughly intoxicating scents of cedar and rain and wool. His hair was silky between her fingers, damp from the rain. His body was flush with hers, his desire pressing against her hip, and she shrugged the blanket from her shoulders, even as she tugged his shirt free of his pants to run her hand along his stomach, her skin to his skin, her body to his.

Sylvan dropped his lips to the curve of her shoulder, and she arched into his touch. "I've wanted you since the moment we met," he said, voice raw with want. "I'll make no secret of it now."

"It's not a contract, Soulslayer," she teased.

He paused, chest heaving, expression as serious as she'd ever seen it. "You tell me to stop, and we stop."

She nodded, emotions crowding into her chest until she could hardly breathe for the heat of it. She backed toward the bed, pulling his mouth to hers as she fell upon the mattress, shedding the blanket on the way, relieving him of his shirt as she dragged him down between her open thighs. Needing him in as many places as she could have him, his skin against hers, his breath hot on her neck. The edges of the room frayed, lost to the focal point of this man.

Sylvan's hand rose to caress her breast, and she gasped, back arching as he worked his thumb in slow circles over the peak of her nipple. Slow, torturous circles.

She could appreciate slow. But she needed *more*.

Neve reached between them, curling her fingers around his cock, reveling in his groan as it hummed into her ear. Already they moved in concert, her hips rising toward his, one ankle curled around the back of his calf, seeking more friction, more movement, *more*.

Neve guided him toward her opening, and he kissed her, long and deep, his tongue tangling with hers.

He didn't ask if she was sure. He trusted her enough to tell him if she wasn't.

He pushed into her, and the world contracted, his name spilling from her lips like a curse. And still, he moved with that aching slowness, his eyes like storm clouds, his body filling hers and then retreating before sinking back inside her. Slow. Deliberate. Torture.

Sylvan pressed his mouth to hers, sucking her bottom lip between his.

"I need," she said, then lost the rest of the sentence when he pressed his thumb to her clit and the world exploded in stars. She cried out, his name fracturing on her tongue, and then there was no more slowness as he drove into her, his breath coming in ragged gasps. Details crowded together and fused, until everything became a sensation—the roughness of his scars, the softness of his hair, the sweat-slicked muscles of his chest, the swollen press of his lips, the scrape of his teeth—until she was made of sensation. Until there was nothing else.

She came apart all at once, pleasure bursting out from her center. Sylvan bit into her neck, swearing as he came, their bodies still joined and trembling. She clung to him as he kissed her, slow once again, their breathing easing into a quieter rhythm. And she hoped, with everything she had, that the world would allow this feeling to last forever.

CHAPTER SIXTEEN

SYLVAN

*T*o say that Sylvan had dreamed of Neve before would have been a vast understatement. Much though he'd tried to deny it to himself, he had to admit now that she'd been there since the moment he first set eyes on her, in every spare minute of sleep he'd managed to snatch, every ill-advised daydream.

Not one of those dreams had captured the sweetness of her body tucked tight against his, the pure *rightness* of watching the slow rhythm of her breath through her parted lips, the curl of her lashes against her cheeks. Nor had the dreams come close to matching the exhilaration of them coming together as they had.

The mere thought of it made his cock stiffen. Ready to do it all over again.

But the sun was casting sleepy rays across the floor, the light already tinged in the barest haze of purple. The onset of the Amethyst Moon.

So instead of kissing Neve awake, as he desperately wished to do, he ran a hand lightly down her arm. That touch alone was almost too much. And when she opened her eyes, that blaze of green looking up at him through sleepy lashes, he nearly abandoned his rational decision in favor of making love one more time before running off to save the world.

But her eyes widened almost immediately, moving directly to the same rays of sun he'd been cursing only moments before. And then she was slipping out of the bed, already in motion. "The Amethyst Moon," she said. "We need to get back to Vunmore and find Darius."

Descended of kings and queens. Of course she was.

All too quickly, they were dressed—he in his clothing from yesterday, she in a simple dress procured by the innkeeper—and heading for the woods. As soon as they were out of sight of the village, Sylvan circled his arms around her waist and reached through the aether, traveling them back to Vunmore. Not to the castle, where any surprise might await them, but to the upper levels of the city, where they could get their bearings and learn what had happened since the disastrous attempt to murder Asperion. It felt like days ago, instead of hours.

They landed in utter silence, the city lurching into place around them as the cobblestones solidified beneath their feet. After the relative coolness of the forest, it felt like stepping into an oven. Or a pot set to boil.

Festival decorations hung from balconies and lamp posts, banners hanging limp in the heavy humidity. Even early as it was, there should be vendors trundling their wares toward the market, bakers readying their ovens for the day, early-rising children already racing out of their doors to play. There should be something. Some*one*.

Everything was still.

Unease crept up Sylvan's spine as he scanned the street, trying to absorb the details. Trying to understand. Until, after a beat, his gaze landed on a human woman.

She stood unmoving outside what he assumed to be her

shop, a kerchief tied in her hair, a basket slung over her arm. As if she'd stepped out of her house to begin her morning errands only to be struck into statuesque silence. She stared into the street with glassy eyes. Unseeing, or perhaps only unresponsive.

And all at once, the rest of them came into focus. Through the window of the nearest building, he could see a man standing in his kitchen, a child to either side. A little way up the street, a young boy had paused beside his push cart.

They stood with straight spines, shoulders back, as though they were watching. Waiting.

Neve clung to Sylvan's arm, fingers pressed tight into his sleeve. He couldn't help but lean closer, to inhale her herbal scent. She was breathing. She was moving. She was well.

"They're all enthralled," she said, her voice catching on the last word.

Deeply enthralled. Humans with their dust-coated clothing, their wares, their red-eyed fatigue. But there were mages, too, their vials hanging around their necks like beacons. He wanted to rip every last one from their throats.

Hand in hand, Sylvan and Neve started up the hill toward the castle.

Eerie was too vague a word for this. As they moved through the city, he couldn't help but feel that it was like being haunted by the living.

The predominantly human neighborhoods were bad enough; he found he kept wanting to flinch away from the glazed-over expressions, afraid that one accidental bump would force them to injure themselves. Though, he supposed there was nothing stopping Asperion from commanding them to do that, anyway. If he wanted, the king could order it of the entire city.

What a river of blood it would be.

As they moved into the mage-dominated neighborhoods, it

was even worse. Every enthralled mage they passed made Sylvan feel sick. The power Asperion would be able to yield through each one, through all of them together, was unimaginable.

A flicker of movement caught Sylvan's eye from a right-branching alleyway, as strange in its own way as the frozen citizens. A cat, perhaps, jumping from an open window. Though strangely, he'd seen no other animals about, either. Perhaps they were wise enough to hide away.

A mage ran out of the alley, his vial secured around his neck. His eyes were wild, his hair unkempt.

When he saw Sylvan and Neve, he stopped. "What the fuck is going on?" he asked. Demanded, really, though Sylvan was willing to dismiss it as fear. Especially when his eyes widened, his jaw actually falling open. Under other circumstances, it would have been amusing to watch him realize who Sylvan was.

The mage bowed quickly, hands shaking. "Prince Sylvan. My apologies. I'm sure you have your reasons. I just... what is this?"

The breath stalled in Sylvan's lungs. The mage thought *he* was doing this. Though really, why would he think otherwise? Sylvan was the Soulslayer, the impossible survivor who wielded every known power, save for one. Sylvan was the monster.

Neve's fingers tightened around his. A comfort.

Sylvan could put on a show that would frighten this man, that would prove what everyone believed about him, thereby keeping them at arm's length. A few weeks ago, he might have done just that.

But Neve knew him for what he was. She didn't see it as a weakness.

The mage was frozen in a half bow, the toes of his boot tapping as if he wanted very much to run.

"Were you at King Asperion's ball?" Sylvan asked.

The mage straightened, dragging a hand through his hair. "I

was ill," he said, though Sylvan sensed a lie. Perhaps he'd been with his mistress. Or, judging by the nervous tick in his jaw, perhaps he simply didn't like being around a lot of people.

Sylvan could hardly blame him for that.

Whatever the reason, Sylvan hardly cared. In fact, he hoped there were a great many more mages who'd done the same. "You should hide," he said. "Get out of the city and get rid of your vial. If you see anyone else awake, tell them to do the same."

The mage didn't need to be told twice. He tore the cord from his neck and smashed his vial on the cobblestones before turning to sprint away down the street.

Sylvan only hoped he'd pass on the message. That Thorne and Dahlia had made it to Jessa and their other allies.

He could practically feel Asp's eyes on them as they made their way up the hill, hand in hand. Watching through the eyes of the citizens who stood like silent sentinels along the street.

They didn't stop until they reached the castle.

When the gates came into view, Neve gasped, choking back a sob.

Human bodies hung spiked on the gates, their faces bruised and bloodied, their clothing stained with blood. Necks twisted at grotesque angles, lips curled away from their teeth as if their last moments had been ones of agony. What had happened here, in the hours since they'd been away?

Sylvan swallowed a wad of bile. "Your friend?"

Neve gave her head a shake. She looked as ill as he felt, her olive complexion tinged with green. "He's not there."

It was impossible to feel relief. Whatever the man was enduring, Sylvan doubted it could be called a mercy. And these people had obviously suffered terribly. "The dungeons, then."

"Maybe he got away."

Not likely, with everyone in the city beholden to Asperion's will. Thousands of spies, ready to answer their king's every desire. Whether *they* desired it or not.

If the rebels had made a move during Sylvan and Neve's absence, if this Darius had been among them—and as their leader, it sounded like he would have been—then there was no doubt in Sylvan's mind that he'd either been killed or captured.

Sylvan would have expected Asperion to hang Darius with his colleagues, to make an example of the rebel leader. Though... Sylvan imagined how it would have happened, how human rebels would have invaded the castle only to be stopped by Asp's enthrallment magic.

All but one of them. The king would have noted that.

"Asperion must have learned of Darius's immunity," Sylvan said. "He'll want to discover how much of a threat it might pose."

Neve merely nodded, expression tight with fear.

Sylvan squeezed her hand, intending to travel directly into the dungeons to free the human rebel. But when he reached across the aether to pull the space toward him, a wall slammed down, blocking the dungeon from his reach.

Sylvan stumbled back a step, letting out a breath of surprise. "He's using another mage's power to erect a shield. I can't travel past it."

It was everything Sylvan had feared. Everything Asp had always wanted.

They ran through the gates, the grisly corpses made even more so by the bowing flower garlands at their feet, the streamers, the scent of pastries mixing with the bitter sting of blood.

He half expected that Asp wouldn't deign to meet them at all. That the king would use the enthralled mages, and their powers, to stop Sylvan and Neve before they could come close to facing him directly.

In the end, though, the man was a performer at heart.

King Asperion waited on one of the balconies that looked out over the courtyard, the one in which he'd staged his demonstration. His con. Below him stood a semi-circle of mages. Evander, with his slicked yellow hair, and Fern, clad in green. Along with others Sylvan recognized from court, their faces blurring together.

No Thorne, though. No Dahlia. Hopefully that meant they were safe.

"You were a fool to return here, boy," Asperion said. "You should have scrabbled away into a snake's hole somewhere. You might even have managed to survive what's coming."

"If anyone could," Neve said, "it would be him."

Sylvan wanted to shove her behind him. To protect her. Still, he couldn't help but feel pride at the way she faced up to the king, shoulders back, head held high. A queen. How had he not seen it?

Asperion's gaze shifted to her, then back to Sylvan. "Remarkable. How many of them are there, then? These humans who can resist enthrallment?"

If any doubt remained that the king held Darius, it was gone now.

"Come down here," Sylvan called, ignoring the question, "and face me directly."

Asperion looked down from his balcony, a thin smile curling his lips. "Why would I risk that, when I control the entire world?"

Like a stone launched from a catapult, Evander sprang from his spot, the usual derision in his eyes replaced by blank nothingness as he rushed to attack. His poison-speech might be useless against them, but his sword was not.

Asperion was toying with them. Testing Sylvan, perhaps, to see if he'd attack his own.

Not a problem. Magic flowed through Sylvan's veins like a promise restored, a swell of power too great to restrain. He batted Evander away with a pulse of air, sending the mage sprawling backwards. Evander hit the ground hard, his head cracking against the cobblestones, sword clattering across the courtyard.

But the rest of Asperion's enthralled army was ready. Fire ignited in their palms in a riot of color, dancing across their fingertips as if in a coordinated dance. Asperion controlling it all.

The mages unleashed their fire, and Sylvan dragged Neve to the ground. Heat scathed the back of his neck as he hit the cobblestones, Neve's gasp of shock loud in his ears.

No time to hesitate. Already, he could feel the crackle of magic as the mages readied their next volley of flames. A group of independent mages would have staggered their attacks, meeting Sylvan and Neve with a constant barrage of fire.

Asperion's control wasn't perfect. And Sylvan could use that.

He reached for his shield magic, meeting the next blast with a solid wall of magic. Invisible, impenetrable. A blast of violet fire splashed against the shield, flames licking uselessly at it. But the protection held.

Sylvan rarely worked in shields. He was used to attacking, rather than defending. But they didn't need to defeat these mages; they only needed to get past them. If he could keep the shield up while they ran, they'd be able to make it inside.

Shields were meant to remain in place. They were walls, not bubbles.

But most shields were worked by mages with one or two other powers. And Sylvan had them all.

Ignoring the fresh burst of fire that splashed harmlessly against the shield, Sylvan reached for the same air magic he'd used to throw Evander across the courtyard. Aiming for the shield, he *pushed*.

The shield pushed back.

Sweat beaded on his brow, his teeth gritted so hard he wouldn't be surprised to feel them crack. The shield resisted,

Sylvan's magic at war with itself as he tried to force the wall into something that would move with them.

Neve was breathing hard, eyes darting around the courtyard as if she planned to make a run for it. He didn't think she'd make it past his shield, but he knew better than to bet against her.

"Wait," he said, pushing the word out from between his teeth. His magic was fighting itself, and it didn't like it.

"For *what*? Until I'm cooked to well done?"

Sylvan stopped pushing against the shield, instead shaping the air into a scythe. He dragged it along the shield, carving the barrier and reshaping it rather than pushing.

And finally, *finally*, the shield gave way, allowing him to mold it into a rough sphere, with only their feet left unprotected.

"I'll hold the shield around us," he said.

Together, they ran. Vines snaked up from between the courtyard tiles with audible *cracks*, the stones giving way as Asperion deployed Fern's green-speaking magic against them. Neve stumbled, and Sylvan grabbed her arm, catching her before she could fall.

The vines caught at their feet, twisting around their ankles and trying to trip them up, to hold them back. Sylvan reached for his own magefire, combining it with his green-speech to burn the vines away. Sparks flared beneath their feet as the vegetation withered, Fern's power sizzling away.

Magic filled his veins near to bursting, his skin alive with power as he maintained the shield, the air, the green-speech, the fire.

It was too much. And somehow, it also wasn't quite *enough*.

The mages' attacks skittered uselessly off of Sylvan's shield as he and Neve darted into the castle, Asperion's laugh echoing behind them. Like it was exactly what he'd been hoping they'd do.

Within the fortress, the halls were quiet. Not safe; Sylvan wasn't a fool. But quiet.

"This way," he said, pulling Neve forward. They might be running directly into Asperion's plan, whatever it was, but it hardly mattered. They had to get to the dungeons to free Darius.

Whatever powers Asperion had waiting for them, Sylvan would meet them with his own.

They rounded the first corner, entering an antechamber where several hallways intersected, baskets of fruit and bread still piled high along the walls.

Sylvan barely managed to stop himself before running head-long into a human.

He staggered back, breathing hard, the magic singing through his veins. Humans filled the antechamber, packed shoulder-to-shoulder and blocking the corridor that led to the dungeons. There had to be a hundred of them, servants he recognized from the palace and people who lived in the city. Innocent, to the last.

Asperion wasn't going to meet them with might. Instead, he'd met them with weakness.

Neve's hands were fisted at her sides, her mouth pressed into a razor-thin line. "Can your shield get past them?"

Sylvan reached for it. Delving. Trying to understand it. "Shields usually stay in one place. I don't have all that much control over it."

The sphere would protect them against knives, swords, and fists, just as it protected against magefire. But he didn't know what the shield would do. He hadn't tested it. Even pushing the humans aside with it might injure them.

The monster they believed him to be would do it. He'd push through the group without thought to whether the shield might throw them into walls or impale them on each other's flimsy knives. He might even wrench Asperion's enthrallment away and latch onto their minds with his own. He'd do what was necessary for the greater good.

But Sylvan wasn't that monster. Now, he doubted he ever had been.

"There has to be another way around," he said.

And then Neve let out a choked gasp. "*Lydia.*"

CHAPTER SEVENTEEN

NEVE

*A*t first, Neve hadn't seen Lydia among the crowd of humans, her face blurred by Neve's horror. As the faces sharpened, Lydia's was suddenly the only one she could see.

The apothecary stood in the front of the crowd. Kind, practical, exasperated Lydia, stock-still and staring. A pawn in Asperion's game. A shield.

Sylvan might think everyone saw him as a monster. But Asperion knew good and well that he was not. And he'd use that fact for his own ends.

When Sylvan cursed, Neve made herself look away, eyes tracing over the rest of the crowd. Flint stood next to Lydia, his back ramrod straight. Beside *him* was the woman Neve had helped with the baskets when she'd first come into the fortress.

"You have to enthrall them," Neve said, voice shaking. He could do it, as easily as Asperion. He could reach through the aether and enter their minds. Instruct them to do his bidding, rather than the king's.

It would be so simple.

But Sylvan shook his head. "I don't do that."

No matter the circumstances. He'd die before he used his power to compel someone else to his will. Perhaps it shouldn't thrill her to know he was even willing to risk *her* life.

He respected human life, human freedom, ahead of his own wellbeing. And she realized that she, too, would rather sacrifice her life than be a part of enthralling others.

She'd been treated as a pawn, by humans and mages alike. She'd chosen to save herself. But the humans her mother had allowed to 'test' Neve had never intended to help the rest of their people. They'd have used whatever they found for their own gains.

"Dahlia told me you can free her when she gets snared in an enthrallment," Neve said. "Can you break theirs?"

Sylvan shifted his weight. "I'll have to touch them." He looked at her, gray eyes flaring. "I'll have to drop the shield."

Neve nodded.

As soon as she and Sylvan stepped forward, the humans *moved*. Not in groups, not one by one, but in a single, charging mob, with Lydia at the front. They were unnerving in their silence; the only sounds were the pound of their footsteps and the swish of their clothing as they rushed to attack Sylvan and Neve.

And then there wasn't time to consider it as a fist flew at her face from the side. Sylvan caught it, sacrificing a strike to his own jaw to grab her attacker's wrist, meeting their eyes with that searing gray gaze of his.

It was the man Evander had compelled to eat the coals. Deep scars now dragged his mouth to one side, his bottom lip pressed into a permanent divot.

Like morning mist banished by the rising of the sun, the man's expression cleared. His scarred lips parted as he looked at Sylvan, who was ducking hits from every side while simultaneously trying to touch his assailants and release their enthrallment, to catch hold of a hand here, a wrist there. A dagger soared toward them from the middle of the crowd, and weaves of air struck it aside it mid flight, casting the weapon harmlessly to the floor.

Instead of running—which Neve would not have faulted him for—the man moved to stand beside her.

There wasn't time for surprise, or gratitude, as Lydia came barreling toward Neve, intent on knocking her to the ground. Or at least, Asperion was.

And then Sylvan was there, his body a shield between Neve and Lydia. He touched the apothecary's hand, then whirled away to meet another, and another. One after the other, their enthrallment dropped away like dried-out husks, allowing the light to re-enter their eyes.

Lydia's eyes sharpened, and she lifted her chin, taking in the scene quickly. Her gaze landed on Neve. "Trust you to be in the middle of... whatever *this* is."

Before Neve could respond, Lydia joined the line, joining them to protect Sylvan as he worked his way through the crowd to free them, one by one. It felt like a miracle. Every single human, once turned, moving to stand on their side. Until they outnumbered the ones who wanted to fight them. Until there were two left, and then one—until the fight was over, the corridor gone quiet.

Only then did Lydia turn to look at Neve. "Foolish girl." She raised a hand to Neve's cheek, her tone affectionate. "What have you gotten yourself into?"

Neve actually laughed, though she was suddenly aware of tears pouring down her cheeks. "There's a rebellion. We need to free the leader."

Lydia raised her eyebrows. "Darius got himself captured?"

Neve blinked. "You know him?"

"Child," Lydia said, "nearly every human in the city is a part of the rebellion. Darius *is* our king, and not only by birth. He's united us. I assumed you knew."

Neve shook her head, not understanding. "I didn't."

But then, she'd always held herself apart. Afraid to know anyone too well, lest they should discover her immunity and try to use her.

"How did Darius manage it?" she asked. "With everyone enthralled?"

"Too long a story for today." Lydia patted Neve's cheek, then dropped her hand. "Don't worry, child. We'll fight the false king. While you free the true one."

Sylvan's fingers wrapped around hers, and they ran deeper into the castle as the humans charged out into the courtyard, ready to stall Asperion and his mages. Armed only with courage and a respite from enthrallment. However brief it might be.

They reached the stairwell Sylvan had used to descend to the ancient part of the fortress. Instead of opening the tile so they could descend, however, he started up the stairs.

"How long will your protection last?" Neve asked.

His mouth was set in a grim line. "A few hours at most, with Asperion trying to break it. Dahlia's was always accidental, and she's careful. So my protection lasts longer."

She decided not to comment on the fact that Sylvan knew exactly where Asperion would be keeping a prisoner of Darius's status. This, apparently, was the impenetrable tower. It would have to be; judging by the look on Lydia's face when she spoke of Darius, she and the other humans would scale the sides to free him, heedless of the risks.

Sylvan stopped at a wooden door about halfway up the tower and pushed it open.

A pair of mage guards stood guard before a second door. A cell.

The guards didn't react to their presence. They just stood there, staring at the door, their vials shining around their necks.

"The humans must be distracting Asperion," Sylvan said. "He can't control everyone at once."

It should have been a relief, but the guards' lifeless, staring eyes made Neve shiver. "Not very practical, is it? Deep enthrallment?"

He gave her a wry smile. "Apparently not."

He moved past the guards, and the second door clicked open. Together, they stepped into Darius's cell.

At the sight of him, Neve's stomach plummeted. The would-be king lay upon a plain stone floor. No cot, no blanket, not even a pile of straw. Just a grated drain in the center of the room that made her stomach turn.

Darius lay with his head pillowed on one arm. The side of his face she could see was red and swollen with bruises, a nasty cut sliced frighteningly close to the corner of his eye.

He didn't move.

Heart squeezing painfully in her chest, Neve knelt beside him. If Darius died, they might be able to bring his blood to the pool. It might even still work to seal the mages away. But Lydia and the others, they trusted him. They needed his leadership.

After all he'd done, he couldn't be dead. He just *couldn't*. Neve reached to touch a hand to his neck, intending to feel for a pulse.

As soon as her fingers touched his skin, Darius opened his eyes. "Are you a hallucination?" His voice was rough, as though he hadn't had so much as a sip of water in hours.

"I'm real enough." Neve offered him her hand, which he accepted, wincing as he allowed her to help him to his feet. He favored one leg, and now that he was standing, she could see that the bruise on his cheek extended all the way across his forehead, disappearing into his hairline.

Darius looked at Sylvan, and Neve tensed. The last thing she needed was a fight.

"You were telling the truth," Darius said.

Neve rolled her eyes.

"About what?" Sylvan asked. "My charming disposition?"

Darius only blinked at him. His left eye was nearly swollen shut, but he still managed it. "You really do want to help us? This isn't a trick?"

They didn't have time for this. "We need to get to the magepool," Neve said. "It's the royal blood that grants us our immunity. We think it will allow us to seal the mages back in the Miragelands."

Darius's eyes widened, hope sparking within them. He nodded, as if no further explanation were required.

"Do you have the third royal's blood?" Sylvan asked.

He nodded again. "The guards didn't even search me."

Asperion had been busy, his ambitions overreaching the constraints of time. Darius couldn't have been in this cell for more than a few hours, the night at most. They'd beaten him and left him here to be dealt with later.

"Take my arm," Sylvan said. "If the shields are down, I'll travel us to the magepool."

CHAPTER EIGHTEEN

NEVE

*T*he pool was hidden deep in the forest.

Part of Neve had expected Asperion's shield to block them from leaving the castle. But when she touched Sylvan's hand, the air *twisted*, and Vunmore's oppressive heat fell away, replaced with the rich coolness of woodland shade. The air was so fresh, she could practically taste the pine and earth on the back of her tongue, and a hint of brine that suggested they weren't far from the sea.

The ground was spongy and uneven beneath her feet, thick moss and leaves combining with layers of earth made from centuries of trees falling and rotting and falling again. An ancient forest, the tree trunks thicker than she'd ever seen before.

Darius released Sylvan's arm, but Neve held on. His muscles were taut beneath her touch. Ready for the next phase of this battle. He looked down at her, expression grave. And then he pointed to an overgrown circle of stone.

Had Neve encountered it on a typical walk through the woods, she'd have dismissed it as an old cistern, or an abandoned fountain left over from a long-vanished estate. If she'd noticed it at all, hidden as it was in this grove of ancient trees, their multi-layered canopies grown together so that only the merest sliver of sky peeked through. Weeds crowded around a stone base, practically obscuring it even from a few feet away.

It was so quiet, even the sound of his voice muffled by the denseness of the undergrowth, the moss, the very leaves themselves.

Even had she encountered this place by chance, she couldn't possibly have missed the heaviness in the air, the thick, thunderstorm-like charge that prickled along her scalp. Or recognized it for what it was.

Magic. As if the place had an aura of its own.

The pool itself was a pupil-black circle of water set within a basin of stone, the depth impossible to guess. It might have been an inch. It might have been a mile.

"Thorne should be here." Sylvan looked around the grove with cool efficiency, noting the details like items on a checklist. As if he'd been here a hundred times before.

Darius was looking around, too. He was still limping, his long hair disheveled and free of its tie. For once, he had no instructions to give. No warnings to utter. "What now?"

The pool stood silent and still, as black as obsidian. It ought to be reflecting the treetops, and the beginnings of purple-tinged moonlight that filtered through the canopy. Instead, it swallowed them against its matte-like surface. No reflections. No ripples. It made her doubt whether it would even feel like water to the touch.

Sylvan had said that they needed his brother's blood to open the pool. But that wasn't strictly true.

Neve turned to him. "We don't need Thorne. *You* can open it."

Sylvan hesitated. Despite his title, she could tell that he'd never really considered himself a part of the royal line. A muscle in his jaw ticked, the lines of his neck alive with tension. As though he still couldn't quite believe that he could be compared with the mother he'd loved so much.

"Your mother was the queen, regardless of who your father might have been," Neve said, gripping his arm. Willing him to hear it. To believe it. "*She* was the heir to the throne. Asp can't open the pool without Thorne. But *you* can."

"That is correct."

Neve spun as Asperion's voice echoed into the grove, the man himself taking another beat to step out from between the trees. As far as she could tell, he hadn't been injured during the fight in Vunmore; no blood marred his face, nor did it darken his hair. He didn't even look tired.

But then, why would he be injured? He hadn't been fighting with his own hands.

"Though I'll admit," Asperion said, "that I've been hoping my son's death will shift the power to me."

Someday, Neve truly would find whoever made these decisions about royal blood and immunity to magic and the ability to open—or seal—magic pools. And when she did, she'd demand some explanations.

Sylvan stepped toward the king, hands fisted at his sides. "Where is he?"

Asperion's smile was a cruel one. "Your brother? He got held up."

The air twisted, magic tugging at Neve's chest and singeing the air, as though this place enhanced its effects. And then Evander appeared, with Fern by his side, Thorne and Dahlia on their knees before them. Thorne's lip was bleeding, his shoulders hunched. Dahlia's dress was torn, but her expression was defiant. As if she planned to go down fighting, to the very last.

Clearly, neither of them were enthralled. Though Evander and Fern certainly were, their eyes clouded and staring. Around their necks, their vials glowed.

And then everything was happening at once. Asperion took

a step, and the air twisted as he reappeared before Sylvan. In one quick stroke, Asperion's hand was wrapped around Sylvan's neck.

A cheat, and the only way he would ever have been able to get that close to the Soulslayer in a fight. Neve flinched, ready to throw herself at the king, but Sylvan held her back even as Asperion's fingers dug visible dents into his throat.

"What good is it to control everyone," Asperion said, "if I still must do everything myself?"

Sylvan's eyes burned with hatred, his aura glittering as his power stirred. His pale fingers wrapped around Asperion's, trying to pry them from his neck, but the king didn't budge.

Even Sylvan could not last forever.

Neve slipped free of his grasp and threw herself at the king. But Fern was already moving. She slammed her body into Neve's, pushing her to the ground. Pain shot up Neve's spine as the other woman landed on top of her, and she clawed for Fern's eyes, kicking and flailing for purchase.

The undergrowth stirred, grabbing at Neve's hair, at her dress, wrapping around her ankles to hold her in place while she thrashed, trying desperately to break free. Off to the left, Darius struggled against his own web of foliage.

A woman like Fern ought to laugh at such a triumph, basking in it. But the other woman remained eerily quiet. Her job done, she rose without bothering to brush the leaves from her skirts and returned to Evander's side. Thorne was struggling against his restraints, Dahlia fighting to rise, their attempts useless against Asperion's power.

But Sylvan wasn't making it easy, either. The king swore, his skin flushing red as Sylvan used his power to fight back. His aura flashed red as he tapped his magic, surely reaching for the king's blood, surely aiming to set it aflame as they'd planned for the botched assassination.

"You underestimate the extent of my motivation," Asp said, voice tight with pain.

Hand shaking, he lifted a vial to Sylvan's mouth with his free hand and tipped its contents between the Soulslayer's lips, squeezing his throat harder to make him swallow.

Thorne screamed his brother's name, falling silent when Evander struck him across the head. He slumped to the ground, motionless.

Neve struggled against the undergrowth, fear pounding against her ribcage as Sylvan, too, went still.

The king released him and staggered back. His hand was red and blistered where his fingers had wrapped around Sylvan's throat. Angry red lines stretched up his wrist, up his arms, the blood magic still working to poison him.

Sylvan didn't move. With the pallor of his skin, he might have been made of marble. All the feeling, the intensity he tried so hard to hide, had drained from his eyes. Leaving them staring, as lifeless and emotionless as cold stone.

Be faking, Neve begged silently. *Be pretending.*

The light in the grove shifted as the moon climbed higher, scattering spots of purple across the forest floor. Asperion wiped his hand across the back of his mouth. He crossed the grove and grabbed Thorne by the shirt, dragging his son toward the magepool. Neve wasn't sure the prince was even conscious.

Dahlia lurched toward them, tears on her cheeks. But Sylvan raised a hand, and a pulse of wind struck her back, knocking her to the ground and holding her in place.

As Asperion dragged his son toward the pool, directing Sylvan's magic while holding Fern and Evander's enthrallments —and, she assumed, maintaining the ones in Vunmore as well— the undergrowth around Neve began to relax.

It was too much. Even the combined power of all the mages had its limits. Perhaps the king was too distracted to remember her. Or perhaps he was too overwhelmed by all the threads of magic he was holding.

Immune or not, she was still just a human.

Asperion dropped Thorne by the side of the pool, chest heaving with effort. The prince didn't move. Dahlia was sobbing.

Neve got to her feet. Her legs trembled, but her footsteps were quiet, muffled by the thick forest floor.

She should run for the pool, should stop Asperion from opening the barrier and gaining access to the Miragelands. From making this connection between the two worlds, with the Amethyst Moon shining and the magepool water he controlled. From returning to the place that would charge his magic with unending power.

He would increase his magic until he was nothing short of a god, and then he'd return here. He'd mold the Vales into whatever he wished it to be.

The world she'd grown up in had been broken. That world? It would be one of nightmares.

But Neve was far too selfish to think of anything other than saving the man she loved.

Asperion was saying something to Thorne, whose eyes were half open, his head lolling against the base of the pool. But Neve didn't listen. She didn't care.

She went, instead, to Sylvan.

His aura was a sickly splash of red and yellow, a dying spark of light swirling slowly through it. Like a match trying to cut through molasses, a torch dampened by the thick air of a swamp. His expression was glazed, his gray eyes locked on the distance. He always tried so hard to hide his feelings. Now, there were none at all.

She had to believe he was in there somewhere. "You would never do this," she whispered.

There was no vial in which to drop her blood, no magepool

water that belonged to him. Nothing she could use to break the spell.

So she placed her hands on his cheeks, and then she rose onto her toes to kiss him.

He tasted of fire, his lips at first unyielding. But she knew him. She knew who he was. And she poured every last ounce of it into the kiss, parting his lips with hers and willing him to *remember*.

CHAPTER NINETEEN

SYLVAN

*S*ylvan dreamed of monsters.

Shadow-black wings and venomous teeth, smoke wreathing their claws as they reached for him, mouths agape. Ready to devour. He thought he was on his knees, but he couldn't feel his body, couldn't raise his arms to fight. He couldn't even scream.

And then, a streak of glowing light.

A shimmerling, cutting through the black, skittering across the wraith's outstretched claw.

The monster flinched back a step.

A second shimmerling joined the first, and then a third, until there were too many to count, the little creatures descending on the wraith in a rainbow of light and color, drowning the night.

Neve.

With a roar, Sylvan pushed to his feet and shoved the wraith away.

CHAPTER TWENTY

NEVE

*N*eve gasped as Sylvan's hands rose to encircle her waist, and then he was returning her kiss, his tongue meeting hers with a fervor they should probably save for later. When they weren't in the middle of saving the world.

"No!" Asperion shouted.

Air exploded through the grove, knocking the king away from the pool. Sylvan's fingers closed around hers, and he broke the kiss to pull her toward it.

Darius met them at the edge, a new cut slashed across his forehead. One by one, they sliced their palms with his dagger, blood springing out from between the parted flesh.

Together, they plunged their blood into the pool.

The surface gave way beneath Neve's fingers, warm and pleasant against her skin. But ripples scattered across the surface and magic flared, a ray of yellow light beaming out from Neve's still-submerged hand. A lick of cool fire sprouted from Darius's.

And when he tipped the bottle of blood from the Etran-born royal, the crystalline shape of a snowflake spiraled into the depths.

Neve had no idea what any of it meant.

Amethyst light burned through the grove, the moon now at its peak. Across the clearing, Fern and Evander's vials shone with magic, as if caught between the moon and the pool.

And then, in a searing explosion of light, they vanished.

No smoke, no twisting magic. Just... gone.

The king remained. He lay half-dazed upon the ground, staring at the magepool with wide-eyed horror. He'd held every card, for so long. He'd murdered and enslaved, willing to do every monstrous thing. And still, he'd lost. He was mouthing something that Neve couldn't make out—it might have been "No, no, no"—as he scrambled back, jaw working.

But there was no one left to control. The mages were gone, their powers vanished along with them.

It was Thorne who crawled to the king, who rose to his knees. And it was Thorne who plunged the king's own dagger into his heart without a word. Only the cold certainty of hatred, burning in his eyes.

And then Sylvan was there, beside his brother. Together, they shoved the king's body into the magepool.

As quickly as it had erupted, the chaos ceased.

It felt as if there should be some kind of benediction. Like a chorus in a play, come to announce that the evil king had been vanquished.

Instead the silence returned, so deep and so sudden that it made Neve's ears ring. As if the ancient foliage had merely folded the scene into its memory, along with every other horror it had seen over the years.

When Sylvan turned to Neve, the intensity was back in his storm-gray eyes. He was breathing hard. "Are you hurt?"

She heard the unspoken question, as clearly as if he'd spoken the words themselves: *Did I hurt you?*

She shook her head, voice clogged in her throat. He came to

her, resting his forehead against hers, and kissed her. "You saved me," he whispered, breath hot against her lips.

"Again," she said.

He ran his fingers down her neck, making her shiver. "Again," he murmured.

Darius stood by the edge of the pool, chewing the inside of his cheek as he stared into it. "I thought the water would disappear."

Neve hadn't given it any amount of thought at all. Blinking, she forced herself to focus on the pool instead of on Sylvan.

The water had indeed remained, still pupil-black, still resisting the reflections of the trees. "How do we even know if it worked?"

Sylvan's arms were locked around Neve's waist, as if he had no intention of releasing her anytime soon. She rested her head on his chest, reveling in the strong beat of his heart as he looked at his bleeding hand. "The Amethyst Moon is still in play," he said. "If the Vales blood didn't seal it, the pool should still open on both sides. And Fern and Evander... they would reappear right here."

He didn't mention the king.

They were still standing at the edge of the pool. Eyes on hers, he held his arm out over the water and squeezed a drop of blood onto the surface.

They waited. Neve hardly dared to breathe.

No magic swirled across the surface of the pool. No light, no fire, no snow. And no mages returned to the grove. The pool merely absorbed Sylvan's blood, without so much as a ripple.

"It's done," Darius said.

"Yes," Sylvan agreed, but there was still a furrow etched between his brows. "Only I think..." He trailed off, gazing down into the pool. "I think you're right that the water ought to have vanished. I still feel a resonance coming from it. As if we left a crack."

"A worry for tomorrow, perhaps," Thorne said. He was standing now, with Dahlia a few paces away. They weren't touching, but her eyes were locked on the prince. As if she'd thought she was going to lose him forever. As if she'd just been granted a second chance.

Whether she'd take it, Neve couldn't guess.

Darius nodded. "Let's go home."

But no one moved. Thorne and Dahlia exchanged a glance. And Sylvan held Neve tighter, gripping the fabric of her dress in his fists. As if he feared she might step away from him forever.

Finally, he said, "I don't think we can."

Neve imagined that yesterday, that sentence would have delighted Darius. Instead, he regarded Sylvan with open surprise, eyes wide, lips parted as if he wanted to protest.

"The humans have to believe that every last mage was banished to the Miragelands," Sylvan continued. "They'll never trust us to live among them."

It was a statement of fact, not an accusation. And still, it made Neve's heart squeeze. "The humans saw you fight in the castle," she said.

Even as she said the words, though, she knew it wouldn't be enough. Those hundred-or-so humans might pass on the story of Sylvan's heroism, but it would soon be nothing but rumor. By the time it reached the country villages, he might once again be the villain of the entire tale.

Darius pressed his lips tight, and he frowned as though if he only thought hard enough, he might come up with a solution. But then he nodded, turning to Neve. "You have your ancestral seat. In Silerith. We'll redraw the borders as they once were, and you can take up your reign there. The lands are rather wild, but I imagine you'll make excellent use of them."

Ancestral seat. *Reign.* As if she knew anything about ruling a country. But then, the humans *would* need a certain amount of leadership. Organization. They'd opened a whole new world.

A whole new *free* world. It made her head spin with excitement. And no small amount of anxiety.

"It would be up to you," Darius added. "Whether to offer them sanctuary."

Suddenly everyone was looking at *her*. Thorne, his face bloody and bruised. Dahlia, hands clasped together in front of her.

And Sylvan. Suddenly, she understood the source of his anxiety. He thought himself so unreadable, so stoic. But Neve could read the hope in every blink, every crease he tried not to allow into his cheeks, around his eyes.

As if she would ever deny them, after all they'd done. All they'd just sacrificed, for the sake of saving her people.

More importantly, she wanted them with her. She wanted *Sylvan* with her.

"You'd be welcome there," Neve said. "With your allies, however many there might be. Any mages who remain. As long as they agree never to use their powers to compel anyone, human or mage."

And then Sylvan was kissing her, hands gripping the fabric of her dress as he drew her closer still, like he needed her to breathe.

"You have a way to contact your people?" Darius asked when they broke apart.

It was amazing how quickly the man pivoted from rebel leader to would-be king. Neve had no doubt that Darius would soon have Vunmore operating smoothly, and with fairness.

Perhaps he could teach her how. Though she supposed it would have to be from a distance.

"We've a network," Sylvan said. "We can get word to them."

Neve's arms were still around him. She never wanted to let him go. "No one can know who they are," she said. "No one can know that any mages remain in the Vales."

177

Darius pressed a hand to his chest. "I'll protect your secret with my life. You have my word."

EPILOGUE

NEVE

THREE YEARS LATER

$\mathcal{T}$he chill of autumn came early to the mountains, but Neve never minded.

She sat on the patio, nursing a cup of hot tea and enjoying the freshness of the early morning air. On the lawn, Thorne was playing a game with her two-year-old son, Kit. She hadn't quite worked out the rules, but it was a scheme of Kit's devising that had his uncle leaping through a series of hoops the boy had laid out upon the grass. All while Kit giggled uproariously.

Her ancestral seat, as Darius called it, had turned out to be nothing short of a castle. A fortress, though it had been half fallen to ruin when they arrived, empty and believed by the locals to be haunted. The few people who'd lived in the area had been suspicious of her arriving out of nowhere to take up her place in it.

But then, those had been strange times. The mages gone, enthrallment a thing of the past.

One didn't simply take a kingdom. Except... well, except when one *did*.

There'd been no one else. And in the intervening years, they'd made good use of the land. It helped, of course, that the remaining mages had retained their powers. Perhaps it meant ominous things for the magepool, for the barrier between the Vales and the Miragelands, but Neve couldn't regret it. Not when their powers quietly ensured that the crops were abundant, the harvests plentiful.

More Sil people moved to the area around the castle every month, too. It was practically becoming a town.

The patio doors opened behind her, and Sylvan appeared, carrying his own mug. His hair was mussed from sleep, and the smile he gave her lived across his entire face. He bent to kiss her, lingering with his fingertips brushing down her cheek. "Your Majesty," he murmured.

On the grass, Kit changed the rules of the game, the hoops rearranging themselves by magic and prompting his uncle to throw up his hands in mock disbelief while the boy collapsed in a fresh fit of laughter. He was already showing evidence of Sylvan's powers. *All* of Sylvan's powers.

He was, in short, something of a handful.

Darius had installed a monastery at the site of the magepool, an order of guards trained to watch for any sign of trouble. Poisonkeepers, he called them. A week ago, they'd awaited the return of the Amethyst Moon with tense fear, assuming that if the mages were to break back into the Vales, it would happen on that night. According to Darius, the entire monastery had stood guard.

Nothing had happened. The pool remained silent, the barrier firm.

On the grass, Kit spied Dahlia approaching with a tray of biscuits and abandoned his uncle in favor of the treats. Thorne bent to pick up the hoops, though Neve suspected he was merely avoiding her.

Some things, at least, never changed.

"Do you think it's closed for good?" Neve asked. "The barrier between the Vales and the Miragelands?"

Sylvan claimed the banished mages would have to take much stronger measures if they wanted to return again. That royal mage blood wouldn't be enough, even if they had access to it. Which they didn't.

He ran a hand through his hair. "If it were truly closed, we wouldn't have access to our magic. But…"

His gaze drifted to Kit, who was chasing after a butterfly, a biscuit clamped in each fist. "But I think we have to maintain our hope."

With that, Neve had to agree.

—✳—

THE END

—✳—

Thank you so much for reading!

Are the banished mages truly gone — forever?

Find out in Book One of the *Poisoned Kingdoms* series, *Winter's Fate*. Available now!

The disgraced captain who hates magic. The exiled princess who wields it. And a realm on the brink of war.

Five years ago, Laena abandoned her crown. Now she lives in exile, tending her garden and hiding a deadly secret: she possesses magic in a realm where it's forbidden. And she's not the only one.

When shadow monsters attack and assassins strike, there's only one person who can help her: Captain Callum Farrow, the infamous magic hunter of Aglye.

He's sworn to destroy anyone who wields magic. She's sworn never to reveal her power.

One touch is all it takes to ignite something dangerous between them. One kiss to make her forget why she can't fall for him.

But as shadow monsters emerge and assassins strike, their forbidden attraction becomes the least of their problems.

Ancient magic stirs in the realm. Enemies gather at the borders. And Laena must choose between the man she loves and the kingdoms she's sworn to protect.

Some loves are worth risking everything for. Some duties demand you sacrifice it all.

Winter's Fate is the first book in a sizzling fantasy romance series where duty and desire collide, and the fate of kingdoms hangs in the balance.

ABOUT THE AUTHOR

Amelia MacLeod lives in Upstate New York, where she spends a lot of time wandering around in the woods and chatting with the trees. (They rarely chat back.)

She love bonfires and ghost stories and all kinds of wild things -- from the cardinal who taps on her window every morning to the bats who swoop overhead at dusk, snapping up mosquitos for supper.

(She doesn't much care for the mosquitos.)

She also loves stickers. And tiaras. And hot chocolate piled with marshmallows.

Amelia writes stories where love conquers all, where characters unlock their true power by choosing love over whatever has been holding them back -- and where that love is stronger than the lies they've been telling themselves.